The Seed Garden

David Reynolds-Moreton

sci-fi-cafe.com

The Seed Garden
David Reynolds-Moreton

sci-fi-cafe.com

THE STATEMENT

IN THE BEGINNING were the PRIME STATEMENT and the DIRECTIVES, and the LAWS thereof, and the WORDS of the LAWS.

And the FIRST LAW when implemented shall condense energy into matter, so bringing about solidity. And the distance between points of solidity shall be called space, and shall thus create time, because of the distance between them.

And so shall come about matter, energy, space and time, and from these the SECOND LAW shall create the universe, and all that it shall contain...

...and the last WORD of the last LAW shall be the driving force of all things created containing a Life Force, and that WORD shall be called SURVIVE...

One:
The Arrival

JED STOOD AT the top of a stony rise, looking down on the shattered remains of the big ship's escape pod spread out before him like so much redundant metal in a scrap yard.

He still found it hard to believe that he had survived the horrendous landing on the planet with only a few minor bruises as the escape pod careered from one jagged rock to another, tearing itself to shreds in the process.

Why the ship's detectors had not registered the oncoming shower of meteorites and deflected them with the repulsion shields, he would never know. The ship itself had been thrown off course and thundered on under full power, the heavy shielding of the engines protecting them from the meteoritic bombardment which had already ripped through the forward section, totally disabling the main control room.

Being the only person on board the giant ore ship, he only had himself to think about with regard to surviving the destruction which was going on all around him. The scream of tortured metal rent his ears at a painful level, and along with the pungent toxic fumes of burning plastic from the control room, which was now enthusiastically ablaze, he was also by assailed by pieces of flying wreckage and sprays of hydraulic fluid from ruptured control lines as the meteorite storm continued to dismember the ship around him.

As the air was sucked out of a multitude of small holes in the ship's hull, it set up a series of screaming whistles, which apart from setting his teeth on edge, further emphasized the need to seek the sanctuary of the ship's escape pod while there was still enough air to sustain him.

The escape pod was the only hope of survival he had. There was no time to think, only pure reaction from long training sessions would enable him to survive now.

With his head swimming from lack of oxygen, and the toxic fumes from just about everything which was combustible in the ship, he staggered into the pod's antechamber, clamping the door closed behind him.

By the time he had fumbled and struggled into the space suit and clamped the helmet on, the pod's door had automatically opened, being triggered by the anteroom's entry door being sealed shut.

Jed crawled through the small entry hatchway into the cramped confines of the pod, pulling the door closed behind him and activating the door's locking device. After plugging his air hose into the receptacle on the side of the control panel, he simultaneously took a deep breath of pure clean air, and hit the pod's release button.

Several seconds later, after the automatics had checked to see if everything had been done correctly, there was a lurch as the holding clamps released the pod and the power unit jetted it free from the main ship.

As the navigation and communication equipment had been the first to suffer the meteorite's onslaught, there had been no time to send details of his mishap, and although the pod had a distress beacon, it was not intended for long distance broadcasting, and he knew for sure the signals would not reach his main base.

If the signals were picked up by some nearby ship, his oxygen might just about last until rescue, but as there had been no sign of other ships in this star cluster prior to the disaster, he realized the chance of someone coming to his aid was on the negative side of zero.

His only chance of prolonged survival was to find a suitable planet on which to land, and it would have to have water and an oxygen based atmosphere.

When his heartbeat had returned to as near normal as it was likely to get, Jed set about looking for a suitable solar system among the myriad pin points of light which might offer some hope of survival in the long term.

The pod's instrumentation was very basic, as it was only intended to sustain life until rescue could be affected. But it did have a small viewing port, and it was through this that Jed scoured the heavens for a nearby sizeable sun with attendant planets.

At the bottom of the view port, a large blue white star shone brightly, and as the next nearest star only twinkled in the far hazy distance, he had little option other than to take a closer look at what was on offer.

The pod had acquired the same forward velocity as the main ship when they had parted company, so there was a considerable forward momentum, thus saving the rather small fuel reserves for manoeuvring, and the final approach to a planetary landing.

As the large blue white sun grew ever bigger in the view port, Jed caught a glimpse of sunlight reflecting off a lone planet as it circled the giant star. It was still a considerable distance away and would take a good twenty time units to get within close sighting distance.

As he had no other options open to him, Jed began the manoeuvre to bring the pod into an intersecting path with the tiny speck of light, resigning himself to the fact it was a chance in a million that the planet would be similar enough to his home world to support him.

There were several 'pings' as the outer fringes of the meteorite storm brushed against the side of the pod, but fortunately the particles were only very small, and no damage was done, although his heart missed the odd beat.

Checking the pod's air pressure matched that in his helmet; Jed disconnected the air hose and removed the cumbersome headgear. Quite some time had to elapse before he would have to take control of the pod and guide it down to the planet's surface, so he looked around for something to while away the time.

The controls were simple in the extreme, being a main drive unit with side thrusters for directional control, and a simple radar system indicating any other objects within the immediate area. He found the distress beacon switch and activated it. The tiny orange light blinked on and off, indicating that the signal was being sent out and giving him some comfort of a sort. It was most unlikely that anyone would pick up the message, but he had nothing to lose.

Satisfying himself that he understood which controls did what when the time came to use them, Jed then located the rations and the water supply, and was relieved to find there was enough to last for at least one hundred time units.

There was plenty enough for the journey to the planet, and once there, a generous supply to keep him sustained until he could locate his own supplies.

The oxygen supply was recyclable, removing the carbon from the carbon dioxide in his breath, and as far as he could remember, would long outlast the food and drink.

With nothing else to do, Jed decided to partake of a little light refreshment. He was more than a little disappointed when he found that the food supply only consisted of compressed blocks of concentrate, which then had to be dissolved in water, making a thick soup.

He found the plastic beaker and carefully pushed in a concentrate block. With the tube from the water container plugged into the lid, he then filled the beaker with water.

Disconnecting the water supply tube, Jed waited for the block to dissolve, but it just lay there, inert at the bottom of the beaker. Wondering what to do next, he nearly let the beaker go as the block suddenly came to life, propelling itself around in the water until it was lost from sight as the pale amber coloured mixture thickened and went opaque.

'Well I'll be damned,' he muttered to himself, as he put the feeder tube in his mouth and took the first tentative suck. It was smooth and slightly warm, and tasted of something familiar, but he was unable to define exactly what it was.

With the soup finished, Jed looked out of the view port for the tiny pin prick of reflected light which represented the planet he hoped to reach. It seemed no nearer, not that he really expected it to be.

He felt surprisingly calm, considering the trauma he had been through, and while going through the recent events in his mind, he felt his eyelids getting heavy. It was an effort to keep them open, so why bother; he had plenty of time before reaching the planet. After a couple of wriggles to get himself more comfortable, he drifted into a deep sleep.

Safely strapped in his seat by the restraining straps, Jed snored his way through the oblivion which sleep brings, entertained by a few dreams which he was later unable to recall with any detail, although he felt sure they had some importance with regard to recent events.

Twice he was nearly woken from his slumbers, as the pod was given a gentle nudge by something correcting the course towards the planet below, which by now had increased considerably in size and brilliance.

A rogue piece of space detritus hit the pod, and the resulting clang of struck metal finally brought Jed out of his sleep and back into the real world, and its problems.

He stretched, as much as the restraining harness would allow, yawned, and looked out of the view port in astonishment. The planet below had grown to almost fill the view port and he would soon have to begin the final manoeuvre into its atmosphere for a landing.

Jed readied himself for the impending task, going over the sequence of events again and again to make sure he had optimised each detail. As fuel was limited, he thought it best to save as much as possible for the final landing, for if he got that wrong, it would be the end of everything.

He decided to let the pod brush the upper atmosphere several times, bouncing out into space for it to cool down again before the next entry, that way he hoped to lose the heat gained from the friction of entry and lower the velocity to a point where the pod would not burn up as it made the final plunge to the surface.

When the planet had filled the viewing port from edge to edge, the first sound of contact with its atmosphere became apparent. A soft rushing noise grew in volume until it became a constant throaty roar, and he could feel the radiant heat from the outer shell along with the occasional creak as expanding metal tried to compensate for that part of the pod which was a little cooler.

A quick burst of the side thrusters, and he was back into space again, allowing the outer skin of the pod to cool a little before allowing it to dip into the atmosphere again.

As the velocity of the pod dropped, the excursions into the upper air of the planet became more frequent and longer, while the buffeting rattled his teeth, and the temperature inside the pod increased to an almost unbearable level.

'I'll probably cook before I land this bloody thing.' he muttered to himself between clenched teeth.

When Jed considered the pod had reduced its velocity enough to make the final dive towards the planet's surface safely, he gritted his teeth and took his hand away from the thruster controls, allowing the pod to drop ever deeper into the thin upper atmosphere.

The escape pod had not been designed for free flight in an atmosphere, and having no wings or stabilizing surfaces, consequently dropped like a stone. Only its forward velocity gave the appearance of normal flight, but Jed knew that would not last for long.

The kind of situation he found himself in had not been covered in any of his earlier training programmes, and he knew he would have to improvise some means of reducing his forward velocity before he reached the surface. The other problem was that as the viewing port was situated on the upper half of the pod; he would not be able to see the ground as it rushed up to greet him.

The feeling of desperation was overwhelming as he realized that what had at first seemed a relatively simple operation had turned into a death trap. He had to land the pod as he could not exist in space for any great length of time, and the pod had by now reached a point where it was free falling towards the planet's surface with no means of controlling its descent.

Suddenly he had a flash of inspiration. Flip the pod over so that he would be upside down relative to the fast approaching ground, and then turn the pod end to end, so that the main propulsion unit would be pointing in the direction he was going, but at a slight angle. This way he would have a view of the terrain below as it sped by, and at the right moment he could use the main thrusters to reduce his velocity just before impact.

If the pod could be held at a slightly inclined angle, it would tend to act as an airfoil section, not much perhaps, but just enough to make the difference between dropping like a piece of lead and a glide.

Somehow his fingers seemed to know what to do as they played over the various thruster controls turning the pod upside down, and then flipping it end to end so that the main thrusters pointed in the general direction of travel.

A slight feeling of nausea swept over him as he viewed the approaching terrain from an inverted position and with his back to the direction of travel, but this was quickly forgotten as the ground rushed up to greet the pod.

At what he thought to be the right moment, the fingers of his right hand danced over the controls, applying power to the thrusters and the main drive, desperately trying to lift the pod from the fast approaching surface below.

With a sickening crunch the pod made contact with the planet, and the screech of torn metal made him screw his eyes up in a vain attempt to shut out the hideous cacophony of sounds which ripped at his eardrums.

What few rocks there were on the plain, the pod seemed to find, careering from one to another, and shedding pieces of itself along the way.

When all was finally still, Jed found himself still strapped in his seat, with a long line of debris strung out before him.

He was bruised and battered, and his ears still rang from the multitudinous series of noises created by the disintegrating pod, but as far as he could tell, he was still in one piece.

Jed's shaking fingers undid the restraining straps, and he slowly and carefully extricated himself from the tangled remains of the shattered pod, hardly able to believe he was still alive.

Standing back a few metres from the wreckage, he could see that his decision to land the pod backwards probably saved his life. The impact on landing would have torn him from the restraining harness, leaving parts of him distributed among the rest of the pod, which now lay scattered in a straggly line within the confines of a slight depression in the hard barren terrain.

As it was, he had been forced back into the seat with enough energy to cause him to nearly black out as the pod hit the ground, and his seat, still firmly attached to the bulkhead, was the largest piece of wreckage in sight.

Before attempting to land the pod, Jed had switched his oxygen supply back to the suit unit, in case he was thrown clear of the pod on impact, and he now glanced down at the suit's gauge to see how long he had left. He didn't.

The gauge now indicated empty, despite his repeated frustrated tapping of the dial. A few quick panic driven steps took him back to the seat and its attendant bulkhead, but there was no sign of the oxygen receptacle.

And then he remembered, it was attached to the control panel, and that could be anywhere. All that remained of the air processing unit was half of the outer casing, and a torn pipe which had once led to the missing receptacle.

His suit supply was on zero, and most of the pod's oxygen unit lay scattered in pieces. Within minutes he would be dead, unless the planet's atmosphere would support him.

Jed realised he had little choice in the matter, slipped the catch on his helmet and took a deep breath of what the planet had to offer in the way of breathable air.

His head spun, and he had to hold onto the bulkhead to prevent himself from falling over, and then he realized he had been hyper ventilating.

Gaining control over his breathing rate, the dizzy feeling eased, and he thought there must be enough oxygen in the atmosphere for him to survive, although it did seem a little low, as he found out when climbing the mound to view the wreckage of the pod.

Jed decided to climb the low mound at the side of the depression in order to get a better view of the rest of the wreckage, as he would need to search every piece for anything which would aid his survival.

From the top of the mound he could see the full length of the depression the pod had chosen to litter with its constituent parts, and again he realized he was a little more than lucky to be alive, and with only a few bruises.

'Better salvage the water and food, such as it is.' He found himself talking out loud, and chuckled. 'Ah well, that's the first sign I suppose.' he added, as he made his way back down the slope towards the wreckage.

He found the water tank behind the bulkhead to which his seat was attached, the flexible supply tube still intact. Of the beaker there was no sign, so he put the end of the tube in his mouth and pressed the release tab. A flow of lukewarm water flooded into his parched mouth, and he drank greedily.

The search for the food concentrates took him back almost to the point of impact. The container was badly dented, but when he had pried the lid off, the blocks were all present, barring the one he had consumed during his flight towards the planet.

Jed felt exhausted after his long walk up the depression to where the pod had made its first fatal contact with the planet, and he sat down to rest and look over his options, of which he quickly decided, there were only two. Stay with the water supply until it was all consumed and then die of thirst, or collect anything which might aid his survival along with the water and food blocks, and head out to see what this God forsaken planet had to offer.

As he trudged back towards the water tank, he found the beaker lying on its own in a clear patch of sand, and undamaged. That reminded him that he would have to find something in which to carry the water, as there was no way he could transport the heavy tank which was still firmly attached to the even heavier bulkhead.

Two severely battered metal containers, which had probably held compressed gas or air, complete with their exit pipes, were the only things he located which were suitable, but he would have to find some way to get the pipes off, and the water in.

Back at the water tank, Jed managed to jam the hexagon shaped pipe connector into a convenient slot in the bulkhead, and, rotating the metal container, unscrewed the pipe.

A quick sniff at the open end of the container revealed no noxious smells, but Jed resolved to flush the canister out with a little water just the same, in case there was a residue of something harmful. The other container surrendered its attached pipe and fittings quite easily, and he now had the means to store what he thought to be about ten litres of the precious life giving fluid.

A means of carrying the two containers and the box of concentrates had now to be found, and he looked around for a suitable sharp piece of metal to use as a knife.

The material covering the pod's seat was tough, but he managed to remove a section large enough to fold in two, and with a length of wire, stitched the sides together to make a crude bag.

The harness, which had held him so firmly during his descent to this new world, was cut from its fixings and wired onto the bag, the whole assembly now resembling a somewhat makeshift backpack.

A long metal tubular strut, with one end hammered to a rough point, would act as a walking stave, a means of safely prodding anything suspicious, and a weapon, should the need arise.

After one more careful tour of the wreck site to make sure he had not missed anything which might be useful, Jed returned to the water tank, and filled the two containers.

Using a piece of firm plastic foam from the now naked seat, he fashioned a couple of bungs for his water containers and loaded them into the backpack, along with the food concentrates and the 'knife'.

Jed drank deeply from the water tank until he could hold no more, and then shouldering his pack and picking up his stave, he took one last look at the wreckage of the pod and headed up the slope to get a better view of the surrounding terrain. He must now locate a local water supply, and something to eat for when the concentrates ran out, but the seemingly endless barren wastes of sand and stone which met his gaze held little promise of either.

The sky held a few thin high altitude wispy clouds, more like giant ghostly feathers than the heavy grey rain clouds necessary for a good downpour of rain, so perhaps there was underground water somewhere he hoped. If not, he was going to be in a good deal of trouble.

The sky was a deep blue, tinged with green near the horizon, while a large blue white sun blazed down unmercifully on a terrain of sand and gravel. The odd rock reluctantly poked through the otherwise barren landscape, but of vegetation there was no trace, and that worried Jed.

Among the sand and gravel were what he first thought to be small pieces of coloured glass, but as the colours covered the whole spectrum of the rainbow, he knew they must be some naturally occurring mineral, possibly what would normally have been considered precious or semiprecious stones.

'God, there's a bloody fortune here!' he said out loud, wishing he could hear another voice agree with him.

The terrain was made up of a series of low rolling mounds which stretched off into the far distance, gradually blending into a line of low hills. Behind the hills, it seemed that dark mountains fringed the horizon, but they shimmered in and out of vision in the heat haze, so he could not be sure if they really existed at all.

Jed had to slow down what he considered to be his normal walking pace, as he was getting out of breath when going up the sloping mounds, and they seemed to be getting steeper the further he went. A faint metallic taste to the dry and sterile air made him wonder if he would ever find any native water, but then on reflection, he had visited many worlds which contained desert areas surrounded by lush countryside, so he trudged on in hope.

The other factor which made him feel uneasy was the total absence of any sound. An eerie stillness seemed to soak up his very footfalls, and even when he vocalized the odd comment, the words seemed distant, as though his ears were full of cotton wool.

The sun appeared to have moved across the sky a little since he had left the wrecked pod, so therefore there should be day and night. He also reasoned there should be a wind, or at lease a slight breeze as the land mass heated up each day, but there was none. It was as if time was frozen, and he was the only thing which moved in this strange landscape.

He had been wise to keep his space suit on, as the metallic finish reflected most of the blistering sunlight which would otherwise have raised his body temperature to unbearable limits, and caused a great deal of water loss.

Jed was almost in a dreamlike state when he reached the top of the last mound in a seemingly never ending series of undulations. Before him, the ground dropped to a flat plain of fine sand before the next line of ridges began. Scattered about on the smooth surface were many brilliant pinpoints of light, which twinkled as he moved his head, giving them a false sense of movement.

As he was heading for the distant hills anyway, he would have to cross the intervening sand plain, and so it was with renewed enthusiasm for something different that Jed hurried down the last slope and onto the soft sand below.

The first of the twinkling light points he came across turned out to be a slender thirty centimetre high triangular black glass-like pyramid, with three perfectly symmetrical fluted sides. The edges looked wickedly razor sharp and he was tempted to test them, but thought better of it.

The three flutes came to a point as fine as any needle he had seen, and he wondered what purpose they served, if any.

Jed looked around for a stone, but the area was just fine sand. Reaching into his bag, he withdrew the piece of metal he had used as a crude knife, and gave the Shard, as he mentally christened it, a sharp tap.

A clear bell like tone sounded, although he thought he felt it rather than heard it with his ears. Not knowing quite why he did it, Jed then ran the piece of metal across the fine tip of the Shard, and nearly dropped it as a loud clear tone echoed around inside his head. The piece of metal now had a deep groove in its surface, where it had been dragged across the Shard's tip, which showed no sign of being blunted.

'What the hell do we have here?' he asked himself, but the words were swallowed up in the hungry silence, so he barely heard them.

Being very careful not to touch the razor sharp edges of the Shard, he scrapped away the sand at its base to see how far it penetrated the sand. At about half a metre he gave up, as the sand kept running back into the hole.

The groove in his 'knife' was just that. No burred edges, just a clean cut, with the metal removed as if it had been machined away. Jed felt very uneasy about the whole situation, but was unable to pin down exactly what it was that caused the feeling.

Surveying the field of Shards, as he thought of it, the idea came to him that the Shards somehow grew, and were advancing into the rolling mounds of sand and gravel he had just travelled over, levelling the landscape in the process and converting it to the fine sand he was now standing on.

If he wanted to reach the distant hills, he would have to walk through the field of Shards, and the worrying thing about that was, were there any small Shards in their early growing stage at or just below the surface, and therefore out of sight? Placing a foot on one would probably cause a massive cut, and he would then be vulnerable to whatever passed for bacteria in this world, and he felt sure there would be plenty to choose from.

Prodding the sand with his stave, Jed very cautiously moved into the field of Shards, and noticed that some were taller than others, and this reinforced his fear of treading on a hidden point.

It took him a long time to traverse the Shard field and reach the next set of rolling dunes, and by the time he did, his throat was parched dry and he felt hungry for the first time on his new world. A quick glance at the sun, and he knew that night would soon be upon this place, that's if the sun went below the horizon.

His legs ached from the long walk, and the tension of the Shard field left him feeling drained. It was time for a rest, and a little sustenance.

Jed took advantage of the next deep hollow between the mounds, and taking off his backpack, removed the beaker and one block of concentrate. A small sip of water made him feel better, and he then added some to the beaker until it was nearly full.

The block lay inert for the prescribed amount of time, and then propelled itself around until it disappeared in the thickening liquid. Jed sipped it very slowly, savouring every drop as if it were his last. All too soon the soup had been consumed, and he took one more small sip of water to freshen his mouth as the sun, now tinged a greenish blue, dipped below the horizon, and the black of night rushed in across the bizarre landscape.

Removing the larger pieces of gravel and small stones from his chosen sleeping place, and scooping out a small hollow for his hips, Jed settled down for his first night, curling himself up to conserve as much body heat as possible as he suspected the night would be cold as in most other desert regions he had experienced.

Despite his aching limbs and general mental and physical exhaustion, sleep would not come. He lay there, looking at the myriad diamond like twinkling stars which littered the black velvet of the heavens, and tried to piece together the events which had led to his present predicament.

He thought of his home, the people he knew and would never see again, and the ore ship, with its multiple automatic safety devices. They had never let him down before. Life aboard the ship had been almost as automatic as the ship itself, and he had often wondered if his presence was really necessary in the first place.

Once the ship had been loaded, and the co-ordinates set for its destination, there was little for him to do in reality.

Sure, he checked the progress of the ship at regular intervals, filled in the log book, noting anything which needed attending to when she next docked to unload, but that was basically it, the ship could have done the journey on its own.

He thought about his friends, whom he would never see again, and the things they had planned to do when next on leave. Also the quite considerable sum of credits he had accumulated from his lonely job on the ore freighter over the years, and the retirement home set deep in the wooded hills of his home world where he could do just as he liked, for as long as he liked, whenever he chose. It was all very far away now, and almost like a dream.

There was absolutely no hope of being found. The freighter would by now have left the star system it had cut across, and because the instrumentation had been the first part of the ship to receive the blast from the meteorite storm, it could be heading in any direction, and probably never seen again, as space was so vast, and man's efforts so very small in comparison.

A soft, gentle breath of air washed around him, as if something had passed near by and disturbed the ever present stillness. A slightly sweet spicy fragrance reminded him of something, but what was it? The stars faded one by one, and then he drifted into a deep and untroubled sleep.

The sun had returned to bathe the world in its brilliant blue white light, but as yet the air still had a deep chill to it, and Jed's bones ached with the cold and from being set in the same position for so long. For one brief moment, he wondered where he was, and then it all came flooding back in one horrific rush.

He was used to being alone on the ship, but this was isolation with a difference. He felt a surge of fear and dread, and then it was gone as he prised himself up on one elbow, and gazed into the rising sun.

Once more the air about him seemed to move slightly, and a hint of that delicious spicy smell wafted past, and then it was gone.

Food. That's what he wanted. The beaker was filled again, and this time the soup tasted even better. A small mouthful of water from his precious supply rinsed the last remains of the soup from his teeth, and he was ready for the next stage of his walk.

Jed hesitated for a brief moment before he climbed out of the depression in which he had spent the night. A small line of yellowish stones lay before him. They ranged from pale amber to deep yellow, in a neat little row.

'How the hell did that happen?' he asked himself out loud, and as usual, the words were sucked into the vacuous surrounding silence, causing him to shake his head quickly from side to side, as if by so doing it would bring the words back again.

'There's no way that could have happened naturally,' Jed muttered, 'and that means something or someone is doing it.' He did not like what that implied. In the absence of any logical explanation, he rationalized that given enough stones in enough space, sooner or later a line would appear by random chance alone. But he was not totally convinced.

The line of mystery stones pointed in the general direction he was going, but he chose to ignore the slight deviation they indicated, and stick to his own choice of direction, but he would keep a vigilant eye open for any other indicators along the way, although finding one would certainly blow a large hole in his random chance theory.

The hills did not seem any nearer than they had been when he set off the previous day from the crash site, but he put that down to the lack of variation in the never ending rolling mounds of sand and gravel he had traversed, as distance without a varied landscape can be deceiving.

The sun had nearly reached its zenith when the dunes gave way to a flatter terrain of gravel with a gentle upwards slope, and he stopped for a drink of water. The temptation to drink deeply was hard to overcome, but he knew if he was to survive for any length of time, he would have to ration himself severely until a local source was located, and so far there had been no sign of that.

Jed rammed the bung back into the water container with a little more force than was strictly necessary, and resumed his walk up the slope, hoping to find a change of scenery at the top. He did, and nearly fell into it.

A ravine, some two hundred metres across, barred his way, stretching in both directions for as far as he could see. The only way he could keep on track for the hills was to cross the gulf somehow, but at first sight, that seemed impossible.

Jed went to the edge of the rift and looked down in dismay, it seemed bottomless, the sides appeared to close in and then disappear in the inky blackness below.

He could feel frustration building up and suppressed it, knowing full well that if he let it get the upper hand it would cloud his judgement. Somehow he had to get across the rift, for there had been no sign of water so far in the desert area, and the hills being a different type of terrain, may well have channelled any rainfall into the valleys.

The rift looked as if the planet's surface had shrunk, and then being too tight for its core, had split, so clean and deep was the break.

Although he was used to being outside a ship in deep space, standing near the edge of the rift gave him a surprisingly uncomfortable feeling, and he withdrew from the seemingly bottomless abyss.

Jed knew he had to confront the rift again, just in case there was a means of crossing it, so he dropped onto all fours and crawled to the edge, going down flat on his stomach for the last metre or so.

He still got a strange feeling as he peered over the edge, but it gradually faded away the longer he stayed there. The sides of the rift were quite jagged, and could possibly be climbed if he was careful, but it would be to no avail if it was truly bottomless or so deep that he would not have the energy or strength to go down and then up the other side.

Jed was about to retreat once more from the perilous edge, when he noticed an anomaly in the vee cut of the rift far away on his left. There was something in the rift, about fifty or so metres down from the top, although at this distance he could see little detail, but it did look as if it might extend from one side to the other.

Two:
The Bridge

Getting to his feet, he set off a few metres back from the edge to get a closer look at what had fallen into the rift, and then he stopped dead in his tracks. 'The yellow stones', and a shiver ran down his back. He remembered the angle at which they deviated from the direction he had taken, and after a rough calculation realized that if he had followed the line, he would have arrived at the blockage in the rift.

What that implied was too much for Jed, and he dismissed the concept, or tried to.

He was hot and thirsty by the time he reached the blockage and crawling up to the edge of the rift he peered over to see what it was. Below the rim, a dark brown, almost black, cylindrical bar shaped object spanned the yawning gap between the two sides. Then he noticed the hole. It was about ten metres from the point where the 'bridge' joined the opposite side, and at the same level.

The edge of the hole gave Jed the first clue as to what he thought it might be. A dark ring, half a metre thick and different from the surrounding rock, outlined the hole, suggestive of a giant pipe.

He shuffled back from the precipitous edge, and sat there trying to make sense of the seemingly impossible. After much thought, he came to the conclusion that somehow two huge pipes had been constructed, some fifty metres below the surface of the planet.

When the surface had split and parted, one of the pipes had broken at the interface of the split, indicated by the hole in the rift wall, while the other one, which formed the bridge, must have sheered some distance back inside the rift, and still being attached to the other side had been pulled out, so linking the two sides.

Wriggling up to the edge again, Jed looked down on the bridging length of pipe, which, if he wanted to cross the rift, he would have to use to get to the other side. He estimated it to be approximately three to four metres in diameter, but it was hard to tell from where he was, as the depth of the rift distorted his judgement.

The idea of walking along the pipe sent a cold shiver down his spine, but far worse was the thought of climbing down the almost sheer face of the rift to reach the pipe in the first place.

A few metres along the edge, the climb down looked a little easier where the rift wall bulged out, but then he would have to traverse horizontally to get back to the pipe. Carefully he visually checked each foot and handhold he would have to use, and finally concluded that it was possible to reach the pipe, but getting across the tubular structure without falling off was another matter.

The journey across the divide would take a lot of stamina and strength, and not a little courage, but the alternative, just sitting on the edge and dying of thirst didn't bear thinking about either.

His parched mouth and a whiff of bad breath brought him back to his senses, and he made up another beaker of soup which he slowly sipped as if to put off the inevitable task ahead as long as possible, and then cleared his mouth with a drink of water from the dwindling supply.

Having checked that his backpack was securely on, he once more wriggled up to the edge of the nerve racking drop into nothingness, located the first foothold he would have to make, and then swung his legs out over the precipice. After a bit of scrabbling about with his feet, he found the ledge and allowed it to take his full weight. It held.

Releasing his grip from the edge of the rim to find the next handhold below brought out a new flush of sweat, but he did it eventually, and he was on his way down to the pipe bridge across the rift.

What concerned Jed more than the steep angle of decent and the difficulty of locating footholds below him was his new fear of falling. It made little sense really, as he was used to being in free fall during extra vehicular activities and never had any qualms about that.

When he was level with the bridging pipe, he began working his way horizontally across the rift face, and came to the hole on this side of the divide. It had been obscured before by an overhang of rock, but now he could reach it on his way to the pipe.

As he would have to pass it anyway, a wide ledge just below the hole tempted him to inspect the opening. Gaining the ledge, he peered in. The surface was black, glass smooth and featureless, and as far as he could tell, perfectly symmetrical. It looked as if the native rock had been fused and compressed outwards to form the actual tube wall, but how this could be achieved was beyond his comprehension.

It was easy to climb into the hole, and he did so, standing upright with plenty of headroom to spare.

'Hello there.' he called out, and multiple echoes came crashing back. So he did it again, just to hear something other than his crunching footfalls on this silent world.

Jed walked up the tube until the light level diminished to the point where he could no longer see the tube wall clearly, and just in case there was a hidden hazard ahead, he turned and went back to the ledge, and the view across to the other side. Somehow it seemed a lot further away than it did before from the top of the rift.

It was only ten metres or so to the bridging pipe, and as he shuffled along the rift face from ledge to ledge, a large piece of loose rock became dislodged and toppled out into the void below. Jed waited with bated breath for the sound of its impact at the bottom, but it never came.

With his fear of falling restimulated yet again, he reached the bridging pipe and was relieved to find it seemed a lot bigger than when viewed from the top of the rift, and the surface had a slightly rough texture to it and not a glass smooth finish like the inside of the other one he had entered.

It was easy to climb onto the pipe, but when he looked across to the other side, it seemed to have shrunk to a quarter of its size. Hoping this was an illusion, Jed bravely began to walk across the rift, careful not to look down over the sides while making sure there were no protrusions on which he could trip.

Roughly halfway across he made the mistake of looking back. A new flush of sweat joined the already soaking wet lining of his suit, and his knees turned to jelly. Before he could help himself, his body had dropped to the surface of the pipe and his hands were frantically searching for something to hold onto.

How long he lay there, spread-eagled and shaking, and cursing himself for his stupidity, he was not sure, but it seemed an eternity. A soft whisper of air drifted across his face, and again he could just make out the faint smell of sweet spice, and then the shaking stopped.

It was a few minutes later before he got up enough courage to stand on his feet and resume the walk across to the other side, but slowly and surely the rift face grew closer and he eagerly grasped the first of the rocky handholds for the long climb up the other side of the divide.

This side of the rift face had fewer handholds and ledges, and was of a more vertical nature, which meant Jed had to traverse sideways in order to find suitable places to climb.

By the time he had reached the top of the rift, he was totally exhausted, soaked in sweat and shaking again, but this time it was from over worked muscles and tension.

He stripped of his suit and under garments, and laid them out to dry in the baking sun. That was when he noticed the most unpleasant smell of his unwashed body. No way was he going to waste precious water in bathing, not that there was really enough to give it more than a perfunctory wipe over.

He would just have to put up with the odour until a copious supply of water could be located.

Jed's body was crying out for water and food as he had expended a lot of energy during the journey across the rift and lost so much liquid in perspiring. A quick swig from the nearly empty smaller water container helped drive home the point that if he could not find the life giving fluid soon he would be in serious trouble.

The concentrate did its little dance in the beaker, and this time Jed drank it down quickly, realizing too late he would gain more by sipping it. One more drink from the container, and it was empty. A little chill of fear ran through him.

The sun was losing some of its heat as he prepared to walk on towards the hills, but first he had to cross the flattened area bordering the rift and then climb the next set of rolling dunes of coarse sand and gravel.

He felt better after taking some nourishment and water, but it hardly replaced what had been expended during the gruelling crossing of the rift. His feet felt like lead as he took the first of many painful steps on towards his goal.

As he neared the transition of the flat area to that of the dunes, he got back into his walking stride, and felt better. The climb up the first dune brought a warning protest from over worked muscles, and he slowed the pace a little to ease the pain and give his body a chance to recover.

By the time he had climbed ten, or was it twenty mounds, he was no longer sure which, the terrain changed yet again.

It looked like pillow lava, but on a much greater scale, and it stretched off into the far distance. Disappointment and despair hardly summed up how he felt. He realized that it would be difficult and tiring to cross, but he had to make the crossing to reach the hilly region ahead.

His first footstep on the pale grey foam like rock nearly sent him sprawling. It just crumbled under his foot, and he was up to his knee in the fine dusty powder. Jed cursed under his breath and withdrew his foot, shaking off as much of the fine grey dust as possible.

In desperation he looked left and right to see if there was a way around the new barrier to his progress, but the pillow lava stretched in both directions for as far as he could see.

Another attempt to cross the lava field a little further along produced the same result, with the added complication that the further he went into the field, the deeper the crumbling lava seemed to be, and could well swallow him up if he went in too far.

By now the sun had settled on the far horizon in a brilliant splash of colour, and nightfall would soon engulf his strange new world in a smothering cloak of darkness, so he decided to stay where he was for the coming night and try and work out a solution to the problem of the lava field.

The beaker was filled again from his last container of water and the concentrate block added as usual.

This time he drank his soup more slowly, but doing so did not increase the enjoyment factor very much as he was preoccupied by the problem of the lava field. A final drink of water completed his evening meal, and he put the containers back into the backpack.

As the light began to fade, he suddenly realized that he had not voided his body of its toxic wastes since he had arrived, and thought he had better do so. Jed's attempt to defecate proved useless, nothing happened, and he only managed a small trickle of urine, and that was a dark amber colour and stank.

His first thought was the possibility of renal failure if he was without enough fluid to flush out the toxins his body produced during the long marches. It was going to be a fine balance between dying from lack of water and kidney failure, so he reached into the backpack for his water container and took another good mouthful.

Sleep was a long time coming that night, despite his physical tiredness, and somehow the stars had lost some of their beauty before he drifted into the first of the worst dreams he had yet experienced.

Jed awoke next morning with a woolly head, aching limbs and a pain in his stomach. His mouth was dry and tasted foul, while one eye was shut tight with an encrustation of dried mucus. He was not a happy man.

He could sense his body craved for something more substantial than the soup-like brew he had been feeding it, and he certainly knew he needed to drink more water.

Breakfast was a miserable affair, despite the extra mouthful of water he allowed himself, and he packed up his backpack with a sigh of resignation and slung it over his shoulders for the long walk around the lava flow.

He had only taken a couple of strides, when he saw the line of yellow stones. It was much like the other line he had seen earlier, only this time there were far fewer stones, and they were nearly all of the same deep shade of amber.

The line was parallel to the lava field, with one end very slightly inclined towards it. He interpreted that to mean he should travel along the edge of the field in the direction he had already decided to go anyway.

'What the hell am I doing taking advice from a line of bloody stones in the middle of a desert where there's no one else around?' he asked out loud, surprised at his own outburst.

He felt like kicking the stones all over the lava field, but stopped himself as it seemed a churlish reaction to something he did not understand at the moment.

Turning to face the direction the stones indicated, Jed began what he thought was going to be a long hike to the end of the lava field, but after only a few hundred metres he came across a small circle of the yellow stones.

'Now what's that supposed to mean?' he verbalized, mainly just to hear spoken words again, and then realized he was taking the stone signs seriously, without a second thought about the rationality of the seemingly impossible.

The only difference in the surrounding area he could see was a raised section of lava, which stretched off across the field like a low wall, dividing the field in two. Did the stones mean him to try and cross the lava at this point? He could see no other reason for the near perfect circle of stones to be there, except as an indicator of some kind.

Tentatively Jed placed one foot on the ridge, applied a little weight, and nearly jumped back as the surface crumbled.

His foot had penetrated the lava for only a few centimetres, and the lava had then supported its weight.

'Well, here goes.' he muttered to himself resignedly, and took the first few exploratory steps onto the lava ridge. The lava held firm, only crumbling to a fine grey dust on the surface, and billowing around his feet at every step.

The sun was by now beating down unmercifully, and with the absorbed heat radiating back up from the lava, Jed was beginning to cook in his own juices, despite the reflective properties of his suit.

Walking on the lava ridge was more tiring than he had expected, as he still did not fully trust the lava to hold his weight, and each step was to some degree hesitant in case he stepped on a softer patch and sank in the grey stifling dust as the lava crumbled beneath him.

He had travelled what he thought was about halfway across the lava field, when he stopped for a drink. The rolling billows of lava now stretched in all directions, and only the outline of the distant shimmering hills offered any hope of a change in scenery, and a possible water supply.

Sitting down on the hot lava, he drank greedily from the dwindling water supply, knowing full well that he should restrict his intake, but the first mouthful was so soothing to his parched and dust clogged throat, he had swallowed three great gulps before reason prevailed, and he reluctantly put the stopper back into the neck of the half empty container.

Getting back onto his feet, he noticed his knees hurt sharply as his full body weight came onto the joints, and he staggered as the searing pain raced along the nerve ways causing a little yelp of pain.

'That's all I need.' He said out loud, a new fear manifesting itself, to be added to that of the lack of water, food, shelter, and the company of other human beings. He managed to keep the feeling of total despair at bay, but only just.

At long last, as the sun began its journey towards the horizon, Jed could see the end of the lava plain, and what looked like a return to the flat sand and gravel of yesterday, or was it the day before? He was losing his sense of time and the sequence of events.

He hurried along the last few metres of the lava ridge as best as he could, and then he was down onto the more familiar sandy ground which would make walking so much easier. Before he realized what he was doing, he found himself looking for a yellow stone indicator, and laughed out loud for the first time since landing.

'God, I'll be believing in fairies next.' he chortled to himself, and headed off in what he thought to be the correct direction, although the rise in the ground ahead obscured his view of the hills.

Before long, the flat level area gave way to rolling mounds of gravel, and the scrunching of his footsteps made a pleasant change for his sound starved ears.

Clearing a particularly high ridge, he saw below him another field of Shards, through which he would have to pick his way carefully. He had gone but a hundred metres or so, when he came across a Shard of a different type.

It was crystal clear, and shone in the now diminishing light of the sinking sun with a beautiful pale blue green luminescence. Not really knowing why, Jed picked up a small stone and tapped the crystal on one of its flutes.

The concussion wave nearly knocked him off his feet, and a brilliant flash of light lit the area around far brighter than the sun could have done. The Shard was now a gleaming black, just like all the others which were scattered about the area, and Jed wondered what had hit the others to turn them black, and if it was still around.

He looked around to see if there were any more water clear Shards, but none were visible from where he stood.

With nothing better to do, he carefully picked his way through the rest of the Shard field, and gaining the next series of rolling gravel banks, saw the hills clearly outlined in the light from the setting sun, with the ominous black mountains silhouetted behind them, their peaks aflame from the scattered light.

They did not seem to be any nearer than before, and he felt a wave of despair wash over him as he realized he had misjudged the distance to his goal, or had been unknowingly going around in circles.

But the yellow stones had indicated the direction to follow, had they not? He could not be sure. Just what were they telling him to do? If anything. Perhaps they were just a freak of nature after all.

As he had thought before, given enough space and enough stones, a pattern or series of patterns, must emerge by sheer chance alone. So much for the 'helping hand' of the mystery entity who indicated directions with little yellow stones.

Jed walked on until the light became too low to travel safely, and then, as the sun finally sank below the horizon in a splash of brilliant colours, he chose a deep hollow between the gravel mounds for the night, and got his beaker out from the backpack for a long awaited meal, of sorts.

The soup tasted flat and uninteresting, and although there were plenty of food concentrate blocks left, the water was running perilously low. He judged that there was enough water for a drink after his soup and enough for two or three more mixes, with a small drink after each. And then, if he had not located a supply, he would be running on empty, and that sent a surge of naked fear racing through him.

Jed settled down in his hollow between the rolling banks of gravel and small stones, finding it hard to locate a comfortable place to rest for the night as there were no sand patches in which to scoop out a hollow for his hips.

The evening sunlight finally winked out as the sun sank below the horizon and the stars burst into existence, littering the velvet black heavens with their twinkling pin points of brilliant coloured fire.

He lay there curled up to conserve his body warmth against the coming chill of the night air, but sleep evaded him despite the aching tiredness of his body. Although his body cried out for rest, his mind was racing, mental image pictures of the past few days flashing by as in a speeded up video.

How had he got into this mess? There was nothing he could have done differently which would have bettered his lot, he had taken all the correct courses of action when the disaster struck, so why had life gone pear shaped?

The detectors should have picked up the meteorites long before they struck, and the deflector screens should have done their job of pushing them off to one side. But they both failed, totally.

It had all happened so quickly, the flight controls and telecommunication unit being the first to be disabled, and after that, the ship's systems were methodically ripped apart, one after the other, until there was no option but to abandon the ship to its fate among the stars.

The main power plant and drive units were heavily shielded at the rear end of the ship, and so would have survived the meteor blast, which meant the ship would plough on through space, off course, and probably never to be seen again. Also, as no distress call had gone out from the main ship, no one would know of his plight.

Jed concluded that if someone had planned his demise, they could not have done so more effectively or efficiently, but surely that was not possible? No one could have gained from such an action, and little was normally done without gain coming into the equation somewhere along the line.

At long last he drifted into a fitful sleep, interrupted many times by lurid dreams of unmentionably unpleasant happenings, most of which were thankfully forgotten by the time the bright light of day began to scorch his already sore eyes, reminding him of his present predicament.

He was surprised that he did not feel hungry, but a raging thirst instinctively drove his hand towards the much depleted water container.

He had though many times of recycling his urine, but what little there was of that was highly discoloured, thick, and stank worst than his rancid breath.

How he longed to rinse his mouth out and be rid of the foulness. Just thinking about copious amounts of pure cold clean water caressing his parched and brittle throat only made matters worse as he recalled the party he had attended just before leaving for his fateful last flight.

The beaker full of soup tasted slightly more unpleasant than the day before, so he thought the water must be going off, not that it really mattered as there was so little of it left now.

Packing up his few belongings, Jed looked around to see if there were any yellow stones indicating the direction he should be travelling in, but saw none, so assumed he was on course for whatever fate had in store for him.

With legs which protested his every move, and a body which ached from top to bottom, Jed climbed the slope up to the top of the mound, and stopped in disbelief.

Ahead of him a vast plain of sand stretched right up to the distant horizon. If the foothills of the mountain range were still there, they were hidden by the band of purple haze which joined the ground to the deep purple blue sky above.

The only features which broke the flat monotony of the plain were occasional rounded mounds of sand, which looked as if something beneath had pushed the sand up to make room for itself below the surface.

Jed's hopes of finding water before his supply ran out crashed. The only thing which had kept him going through the torturous journey from the shattered escape pod was his high degree of self determination to survive, and now it had almost been reduced to zero by the seemingly endless plain of sand.

With a whimper of despair, he relinquished the over riding control over his body, and it slumped to the ground in a tangled heap.

Hot tears of desperation should have flooded down his dry and blistered cheeks, but all the tear ducts could manage was to squeeze a small amount of a thick gelatinous goo out of the corner of one eye, and that only served to distort his vision still further.

Frustration and burning anger gave way to deep and utter despair as he realized the hopelessness of his situation, and as far as he could see, there was no way out of a slow and pain racked death under a blistering and merciless sun.

'Sod this,' he managed to croak through split and peeling lips, 'I'll have a drink.'

As he forced his arm around to get at the backpack, a waft of feted air escaped from his otherwise pristine silver suit and found his nostrils, causing an empty stomach to try and regurgitate the emptiness itself.

Jed realized his fingers were going numb, as he tried to get the bung out of the water container and raise it to his lips. The lukewarm water tasted only a little better than the foulness in his mouth, but at least it was wet, and to a small degree, soothing to his parched throat.

His lips burnt with fire as some of the water found its way into the myriad of cracks in the swollen and split skin, and he winced as the pain tore across the rest of his face.

Greedily he sucked the last few drops of warm water from the container, and returned the bung from force of habit rather than reason.

Jed straightened his pain racked body a little, to get it as comfortable as possible on the burning hot sands, while one hand idly sifted through the silver grains almost of its own volition.

Suddenly he felt something. It was hard, heavy and surprisingly cool. He tried to turn his head to see what it was, but the neck muscles refused to respond, so he put all his effort into swinging his arm around and raising it in front of his face. At first, his eyes refused to focus, but when they did he saw what looked like a bright yellow piece of glass, but somehow he felt sure it was more than that.

The sunlight sparkled off its scintillating multifaceted surface with an almost hypnotic effect, and as he concentrated on the tiny dancing beams of yellow light, he felt the intense pains in his body ebb away to a more bearable dull background ache.

Jed's eyelids felt like lead, and slowly they ground shut over his dry and itching eyeballs. He thought he felt a very soft waft of cool air drift over his face, and the faintest hint of that spicy smell, and then he was falling into a black hole of nothingness, and slept.

When he awoke, Jed had to prise his eyelids open with his finger nails, as the mucus had dried in the heat of the sun and gummed them tightly shut. Gradually they came back into focus, but all he could see was the never ending sand and the shimmering heat haze which caused the odd few distant sand mounds to dance about like tormented jellies.

His body felt numb, but the limbs moved as he found out when he tried to sit up. The overall pain was still there, but only at a background level and he felt he could cope with that as long as it got no worse.

It took a considerable effort, but he got to his feet and took a few tentative steps forward. He was mobile again.

Feeling there was little point in staying where he was, he decided to walk on towards the horizon while he was still able to do so, and it was at least something to do and would take his mind off the inevitable end, which was probably not too far away.

Jed reached the first of the sand mounds, and after kicking the top layer off, it proved to be just that, a mound of fine sand, heaped up in a hemisphere. It was some time later, while he was trying to come to terms with his newly found strength and freedom from acute pain, that he came across the remains of the fossil trees.

Littered about on the sand for several hundreds metres, were what appeared to be the broken branches of some kind of plant like growth. Jed picked up a piece and was surprised to find it weighed far more than he had expected. It seemed to have the remains of an outer layer, or bark, but his finger nails were not strong enough to remove it, and one finger nail broke off during the attempt. He threw it down among the other pieces, and they each rang with a metallic sound as they took up their new positions on the plain.

Jed marched on towards the horizon, and the haze having lifted a little enabled him to see the outline of the hills he was heading for, and this renewed his sense of purpose.

After several kilometres, the pain in his stomach was the first to return. It made its presence felt by a burning sensation deep within his groin, and slowly spread upwards until every step was agony.

His silver one piece suit was blown out into a huge bulge at the middle as trapped intestinal gasses, unable to vent naturally, gradually built up due to fermentation and the general breakdown of his inner workings.

With the now useless food concentrate blocks, no water, and an ever increasing level of pain, he felt like giving up again, but something kept him moving on in what he thought was the right direction.

Several times he thought he smelt the faint spicy smell on the air, and each time the pain lessened a little and for that he was grateful, but deep down he knew he would never make it to the hills.

'Who ever you ar ...' He tried to contact whatever it was he felt sure was helping him, but the words came out as an unintelligible growl, and he gave up as his throat hurt too much. Was anything really helping him? Or was it just imagination born of the desperate situation he was in?

He had long passed the last of the sand mounds, and the terrain had changed yet again to a gently undulating stony plain, like the huge mid ocean waves he had seen when a young lad on his home world.

This made travelling much more difficult, as climbing even the gentle slopes taxed his fast failing body almost to its limits, and he knew he would not be able to keep going for much longer.

When the hallucinations began, they were at least a slight diversion from the ever increasing pain of his failing body as it stumbled along towards a goal he knew deep down he could never reach.

After a while, the hallucinations became more realistic and probable, and it was becoming difficult to tell what was really real, and what was a product of high toxin poisoning and a mind which could no longer take the strain of what assaulted it.

At first, he was completely fooled by the sight of water, it was so real. A large shimmering lake suddenly appeared, and he could almost smell the water and hear the reeds rustling along its shore. He pushed his body even harder, but the water seemed to retreat ahead of him until he finally realized it was a figment of a tormented mind trying to find some solace in a mental image picture, as reality was becoming too much to bear.

Although bitter disappointment hit him a sledgehammer blow, he kept going, and then there were green covered hills and trees, and the sound of distant voices. Jed only just managed to hold on to his sanity, the hallucinations being so real and the frustration and disappointment so great when he realized the truth of what he was seeing.

Desperately he tried to hang on to the only two things he knew to be real, the agonizing pains in every limb and the crunch crunch of his feet on the crystalline sand and gravel as he doggedly forced his body to walk on.

He nearly fell when a searing pain rippled through his lower body. With a sound of tearing cloth, the entrapped gasses within his abdomen broke free and the nauseous odours escaped from the neck of his suit with a whoosh to assail his nostrils.

He plodded on in a dream, but no dream could duplicate the hopelessness and agony he felt. Every step caused a new surge of pain to ripple through his slowly dying body as he mechanically drove his protesting legs forward.

Suddenly his colour vision was gone, everything was now in shades of black, grey, and white, and that was blurred.

Desperately he tried to blink his stiffening eyelids to clear his vision, but the stab of pain he got for his troubles made him cry out involuntarily as they rasped across his dry eyeballs, the thickened mucus which passed for tears having failed to remove the embedding grains of sand.

For a few moments he seemed to be drifting in another state, and the pain was much less. Perhaps he would make it after all. And then he snapped back into the horrors of reality, the agony of his tortured body returned three fold as he stumbled and fell.

The relief of not having to move was almost joyful, the pains seemingly easing away into the background of his consciousness. The only sound was the erratic thumping of his overworked heart, beating like a frenzied drum.

He knew he had to get up, but his body was made of lead and weighed several tonnes. He screamed as he forced himself upright and staggered a few faltering steps forward, only to fall again, twisting sideways as he did so.

A sharp stab of pain screamed in the middle of his back, and he was transfixed to the ground. The pressure and pain in his head eased as his blood pressure dropped.

'Surely it's not night already.' he thought, as his vision finally gave up. All he could see were the swirling stars, 'God, they're beautiful.' he thought, trying to make his dry and parchment like face smile. And then the stars went out, and there was nothing.

As it crossed the Stone Plains, the Visitor was slowly dying from lack of Life Fluid. One by one, its System's Mechanisms failed, until it lost stability, and fell to the ground impaling itself on a Pulse Crystal, causing it to discharge.

The thick red liquid, which was a vital part of the Visitor's operating system, slowly flowed down the flutes of the Pulse Crystal, to soak into the sands beneath.

As more of the liquid left the Visitor, it permeated ever deeper into the sands, finally touching the Spore, which had been lying dormant for aeons of time.

Sensing that the liquid contained Life Fluid, Spore absorbed it quickly, rapidly replicating Link Cells. Gently, Spore then sent a thin Seeker thread up through the flow, to find its source.

Locating the Visitor, the Seeker thread entered, and split into a myriad of fibrils, spreading into every possible corner. Seeker then grew in diameter and modified the outer layer to form a protective sheath. The precious liquid was then processed and drawn down to

Spore, who then sent a coated Probe thread down through the sands, the cracked rock layer, and ever deeper, to find the Life Fluid which was known to be stored in the Deep Sands.

Probe found it, in huge quantities, just before running out of Cells, and after modifying its outer skin to take the pressure, pumped the invaluable fluid back up to Spore.

With cells growing and splitting at a prodigious rate, Spore soon reached full size, and sent a wave of gratitude up to the Visitor. Life Fluid was then pumped up to replenish the Visitor, but in Spore's present state it was unable it to repair the Visitor's damaged Mechanisms. Spore sadly withdrew, and quietly went into its Metamorphic Cycle.

Three:
The Awakening

HE WAS AWARE of being aware, and that was all, there was nothing else. There was no sensation of time or space, just a sense of being. Somewhere. The nothingness slowly turned into a blackness, a total absence of light, which then lightened to a dark misty grey. A horizon appeared, with darkness below it and lightness above. The mists of greyness swirled and reformed, and then his vision returned.

The barren sandy plain stretched out to the horizon where it met the brazen light of the sky with its scorching blue white sun. Below him he could see a crumpled silver form with a scintillating black spike protruding for a few centimetres out of its middle. And then his memory flooded back, revealing with stark reality what had happened.

He realized the pathetic twisted shape below him had been his body, and it was now thoroughly deceased, but he still existed. He could see and hear, as he noticed the tiny rustle of a few sand grains trickling down a slope as they had warmed and expanded under the blazing heat of the sun.

'Well, if this is death, it's not too bad,' he thought with a mental chuckle. He felt free; there was no hunger, thirst, or pain. His vision had a clarity about it he found hard to believe. Every tiny detail of what he looked at seemed magnified, yet still in proportion to the overall scene.

Jed looked back along the way he had walked before 'it' had happened, and he was suddenly hovering over the foamed lava waves he had so much difficulty in crossing.

He was unaware of having moved. One moment he was looking down at the body he once thought he was, and then he was here, some many kilometres away.

'That's the way to travel,' he thought, and wished he could share the revelation with someone else.

Jed was just beginning to recall the crash site of the escape pod when he felt something gently touch him, the hint of a mental tug, and he was back looking down at his old body on the sand plains.

He realized that something had called him back, was it the body? He did not think so, as it was without life, yet it still intrigued him. As he looked at it, he seemed to drift closer, and knew or sensed that every drop of moisture had been drained from the supine form, even the tissues had been broken down to release their tiny amounts of water.

Several times he tried to leave the area, but he could only go a few kilometres in any direction before he was gently drawn back, and that attracted his interest. Not that he really minded, but he wanted to know what was in control of his wanderings.

The sun had cycled around the planet many times, and yet Jed still had no sense of time passing, and that also intrigued him. Nothing seemed to have any great importance anymore, and that was totally alien to his old way of thinking.

It was while he was musing on such things, that he noticed a tiny brown twig-like shoot protruding out of the sand next to his old body, where there had been nothing but sand before. It was only a few centimetres high, but somehow he knew it was alive.

He watched with interest, as at each cycle of the sun it had grown a little, until the tip split into two branches, and these in the passing days, split yet again. Soon there was a plant some two metres high sprouting out of the barren sand, and he thought maybe his old body's moisture had triggered the growth of a dormant seed.

But where was the extra water coming from for the sustained growth which was now well underway?

The plant grew at a prodigious rate, and Jed referred to it as a tree, for the trunk was nearly two metres in diameter and the topmost branches cleaved the sky at thirty.

His wanderings from the tree were still restricted, but he did not mind too much, as watching the tree grow and change in character amused him.

The branches had a tough rubbery look to them, but he was unable to feel them to confirm his thoughts on the matter, and that was one thing he missed, the sensation of touch.

It was a small price to pay for his extended life without misery, but he still missed the sensation of touch.

One morning, just after the sun had warmed up the chilled sands of night, the tree produced a myriad of small buds on the end of most of its upper branches. Jed watched fascinated, to see what would happen next.

The buds grew in size and then unfurled to form a round metallic looking leaf, the surface of which had a faint crystalline structure. At the base of each leaf, a new bud formed and grew to form a stalk which ended halfway along the leaf and a few centimetres above its surface.

Each leaf assembly, as it formed, swivelled around on a knuckle join until the stalk was hanging downwards, and then a tiny drop of clear liquid exuded from its end to form a spherical transparent ball. The ball grew in size, seemed to shimmer for a moment, and then with a faint metallic tinkle, split in two, one half remaining on the stalk, the other falling to the sands below.

The leaf assembly then slowly swung up again until the sunlight was caught by the lens and focused onto the centre of the leaf.

Jed could hardly believe what he had just witnessed; the tree had made its own solar cells and condensing lenses.

Jed looked on in amazement as the last of the solar generators swivelled up to catch and then follow the sun as it climbed higher into the sky.

He drifted back from the tree a little, while he tried to digest what he had just observed. At first he could see no reason for the tree to produce such devices, and far less understood how it was able to do so. He came to the conclusion that perhaps the tree was using the electrical flow to extract minerals from the ground by electrolysis; after all, man had been doing so for ages. The following morning, the tree produced more buds on its middle branches, which then developed into large dark green spheres. The outer skins eventually split into four sections, curling back to reveal a closely packed core of white threads.

The sun rose higher, and as the heat built up the threads expanded out to form fluffy white balls. Jed moved in a little closer to see if he could fathom out what they were for.

As the fine white threads straightened and stiffened in the heat of the sun, he could see that not all threads were the same. Some were of a pale grey colour, and from these, tiny sparks could be seen leaping across to the pure white ones.

It suddenly came to him in a flash. Tree was 'fixing' nitrogen from the atmosphere, most likely to use as part of its building material.

For a moment he wondered why he was accepting such bizarre creations as relatively normal, when not long ago he would have rejected the concepts as totally ridiculous. But he had accepted the fact that he existed without a body.

Perhaps it had something to do with the fact that he no longer had a physical body, and was therefore not hidebound by fixed considerations which had always been used to assess such things in the past.

As Tree continued to grow, Jed found he was able to wander a little further each day. Whether the two things were related, he had no idea, but there was still a limit to which he could roam before being called back, as he thought of it.

On one of his travels, he noticed a massive dark structure on the hazy horizon, but he was unable to reach it, or get near enough to see clearly what it was.   Because of its symmetry, he thought it might be some kind of building, but its sheer size made that a little improbable.

Returning from one of his wanderings, Jed noticed that Tree had grown a large bulge near its base, and curious to see what was going on, he moved nearer. The growth was about three metres high, and stood out from the main trunk for half a metre, and although the same colour as the trunk, it had a series of indentations running from top to bottom.

Jed felt strangely attracted to the bulge, and went even closer to inspect its surface for a clue as to what it was for, and that was when his vision went. He was in total darkness and unable to move for a few moments, and then he could 'feel' again. There was a slight pressure on his back, and when he tried to turn his head to see what it was, it rubbed against something soft and spongy.

After the initial flash of panic, he applied reason to the situation. It seemed unlikely that Tree would do anything to harm him, so he thought it best to just stay still and see what happened next. He did not have long to wait.

There was a ripping noise, as if a strong piece of cloth had been torn from end to end, and then light flooded into the cavity. He was looking straight out onto the sandy plain, but his vision was not quite as sharp as it had been.

Jed tried to turn his head to one side, but it was stiff, although it did turn when he really concentrated on it.

Jed could hardly believe what had happened. Tree had grown a body for him, and put him in it, but he was not too sure he wanted one now.

He got the feeling that he should leave the womb-like cavity he was in, and tried to move forward. There was a squishy plopping sound as he pulled his back away from the mould-like surface within Tree, and he tottered out into the open once more.

The body moved stiffly, and several times he nearly fell over as he tried to get used to this new form of locomotion.

All the joints seemed to be in the right place, although some would not swivel around quite as well as those on his old body. The skin was very hard and inflexible, contributing to the stiffness he felt when he tried to move.

He tried to run, but it was almost impossible as he could not move his limbs fast enough, and fell down twice before giving up on the idea.

All things considered, he felt he would rather be in his free state, unless Tree could somehow modify his new vehicle.

Although he was grateful to Tree for trying to provide him with a body, it was insufficiently functional as far as he was concerned, and he mentally ran through the modifications which would be needed to make it more manageable.

He was leaning against Tree while he mused over the alterations he would have liked, when the birth cavity opened with a ripping sound, and he fell in.

Once more the darkness and the sensation of nothingness. He had no idea how long it lasted, but without warning, Tree opened the chamber once more and he had to screw his eyes up to reduce the blaze of light from without. This time he stepped out relatively gracefully from the birth chamber, and turned to see the lips of the cavity heal over.

Within minutes the natal bump in Tree's trunk had reformed itself to become part of the normal trunk again, and Jed got the uncanny feeling that he was now stuck with what he had got.

The skin was still tough, but it was now of a more rubbery consistency, and certainly more flexible. The joints all worked, and he stayed upright when he tried to run.

His fingers flexed when he tried them, as did the odd looking toes on his feet. All the necessary bits and pieces seemed to be present, except one, the dibber with which the seed of man was planted, but he thought he would have little use for it here anyway. But then how would he urinate? Perhaps Tree had thought of that too, time would tell.

He ran one hand over his head, there was no hair. Perhaps he had no need of hair; there was certainly no trace of it anywhere else on his new body.

Jed thought it silly, but he wanted to thank Tree for its efforts, and not knowing what else to do, wrapped his arms around the trunk in gratitude. He was not too sure, but he thought he felt a slight tremor ripple down the massive growth, but after a while, he put it down to his imagination.

After putting his body through every gruelling test he could devise, he came to the conclusion that it was stronger, quicker, and more agile than his old one. When running across the plain he was surprised to find he did not get breathless, and although there was a limit to the velocity he could achieve, it was certainly far greater than before.

Jed returned to Tree as the sun began to kiss the distant horizon, wondering how he would replenish his body's fuel needs, when a nearby low branch caught his attention.

A yellow plum like fruit dangled from a thin stalk at the branch's end, and his hand instinctively reached up for it.

As his fingers were about to close around the fruit, it dropped into his outstretched hand, and then he knew where his food would come from.

The paper thin skin burst asunder as he placed the fruit in his mouth, releasing a smooth pulp which slid down his throat most pleasantly. The sweet aromatic flavour lingered on his taste buds for some minutes, and he was tempted to search for more, but his hunger had been satiated.

Jed wondered about something to drink, and went up close to the trunk thinking about water, as he was now convinced that Tree could pick up his thoughts somehow. Tree offered nothing, so Jed assumed that the fruit contained all the necessary moisture he needed, and left it at that.

As the days passed, Jed went further afield, and noticed after one particularly long journey the old feeling of having to return to Tree was now absent. Or was it? He could not go too far, as he would have to return for the life giving fruit Tree provided. He was not quite free yet.

How Tree had picked up his thoughts about his new body still intrigued him, and he felt he should be able to work out the mechanism involved somehow. After spending the best part of half a day pondering on every aspect of the subject, it all fell into place.

He thought in pictures, if he tried to add up two numbers, he 'saw' them mentally, if only briefly. 'So that's how it works.' he thought, wishing he could vocalize. He had tried to talk out loud, but the necessary vocal cords seemed to be missing, or he was unable to operate them correctly.

One other thing still mystified him to some degree, that being how he was able to take over a manufactured body, and control it. He almost felt 'at one' with it, as he had his old body so long ago.

It took him several days to inspect all the old theories he could remember, and most of them he rejected as pure supposition. It was when he recalled 'thinking' when he had no body, that it all fell into place.

'If I can think when I don't have a brain, then what's a brain really for?' This cognition was the breakthrough.

Having established the fact that it was 'him' that did the thinking, and also remembering, it only took a short while for the next major realization to manifest itself.

'The brain must be the device which translates the body's sensory perceptions into signals which I can pick up, and therefore 'feel' what the body feels. Small wonder most people think they are bodies.' He realized.

His thoughts raced on, concluding that the main purpose of the brain was to couple him into a body in much the same way a factory was linked to the outside world via its videophone link, and the 'brain waves' the scientists all raved about were not the brain thinking, but the energy flow through the transfer points. To Jed, it all made sense, and answered most of the questions he had stacked up since being on the planet.

One thing would not quite resolve though. If Tree could see his pictures and understand them, then Tree must be more than a mere plant, and that implied it had a 'being, or some kind of awareness'

Jed's thoughts expanded out to consider other life forms, and he wound up with more questions than he began with, and very few answers, so he shelved his theories for a while, and put his attention back on the present.

He wanted to see what the large dark feature on the horizon was, but it was too far away for him to reach in two days, and he considered that was the longest time he could go without food of some kind, and survive.

Jed wondered if he could persuade Tree to produce more than the usual single morning and evening fruit, and perhaps not quite ripe as they split open so easily.

He sat down that evening with his back up against the trunk, and constructed his 'pictures' of what he wanted to do, along with the request for extra fruit, and a possible means of carrying them. There was no response from Tree that he noticed, and only the single fruit was offered as the sun slid down to the horizon for the night. Tree did not want him to leave just yet, he concluded thoughtfully.

Early one morning, several days later, Jed thought he had been dreaming. It was a bit hazy and inconclusive, but he got the general impression that he was to look for a clear Shard, and bring it back to Tree. He then realized that it was quite possible Tree was trying to communicate with him.

After his morning fruit, Jed stood looking out across the plain hoping that Tree would give him some indication of which direction to search in for the Shard, but nothing was forthcoming that he was aware of.

Jed set off for the lava field, remembering that he had seen Shards somewhere close to that area before, and thought it the most promising place to search.

He came across a few Shards before he reached the pillow lava, but they had all turned black, innocently sparkling in the early morning sun like dark glistening fingers, belying their terrible sharp cutting edges and vicious points.

When he attempted to cross the lava at the ridge he had used previously, he noticed his feet sank in a little deeper than before, and concluded that his new body must weigh more than the old one did, and therefore he was probably larger, but as he had nothing against which to compare his new body, he was not too sure.

The sun had climbed to its zenith in the deep blue sky by the time Jed had located the Shard field, but every one had been discharged, and turned into its glistening black stage.

On the very periphery of the field he found the clear Shard required by Tree, and began to carefully scrape away the sand and fine gravel from its base. Half a metre down, he found the Shard's base, but the sand was compacted almost to the consistency of concrete, and difficult to remove.

Fearing the ends of his fingers would be worn away on the abrasive material at the Shard's base, Jed had to leave the Shard field in order to find a piece of stone big enough to act as a scraper, and having found a suitable flat one, hurriedly returned to continue his excavation.

The growing base of the Shard was much larger than he expected, and consisted of a hard hemisphere of sand and gravel which had somehow been cemented into a lump, and probably weighed as much as the sparkling Shard above it.

As Jed strained to lift the mass from its hole, he realized it might be too heavy for him to carry any great distance, and especially across the lava field where the combined weight of his prize and his own not inconsiderable mass would cause the foamed lava to collapse even more.

As he rested the complete Shard and base on the ground to ponder his next move, he heard a faint crackling noise, and the formally solid lump on the end crumbled back into the sand and gravel which had earlier surrounded it, leaving the glass clear Shard free of its cumbersome base.

The Shard was now of a weight which Jed thought he could easily handle, and he picked it up very carefully to avoid being cut by the razor sharp flutes. The sunlight caught the Shard, and Jed was almost hypnotized by the interplay of the reflected and refracted prismatic fires within the crystal.

The journey back to Tree was long and tedious, as Jed went at a slower pace to make sure he did not trip or drop the precious Shard.

The sun had dipped close to the horizon in its usual blaze of colour as Tree came into sight, and from his vantage point on the top of the last slope down to the plain where Tree grew, he could see that it had been busy in his absence.

Protruding out from the centre of the top branches a tall stalk rose up some six metres, on top of which a large golden yellow pear shaped object shone brightly like polished gold in the fading sunlight.

Jed's first thought was this might be a flower bud, or even a seed pod, but it looked unnecessarily large for such a purpose, and he wondered how he could ask Tree what it was for, not that he really expected to get an answer.

He almost gave a sigh of relief as he placed the Shard close to the massive trunk and sat down. What would Tree do with it? He could only sit and wait.

Glancing up, Jed noticed Tree had dipped one of its lower branches, and glistening on the end of it was his evening meal. He could not be sure if it was his imagination or not, but it did seem a little bigger and more tasty than ever, or perhaps he was a bit more hungry after his excursion to the Shard field.

As the sun slipped below the horizon with its final display of flashing colours, the jet black of night swept silently across the alien landscape like a soft velvet cloak, inviting the diamond hard brilliance of the stars to share the dark hours with it.

Jed never tired of looking at these distant fiery suns, endlessly speculating on what other bizarre life forms might exist on their encircling planets.

Next morning Jed thought he could hear movement within the massive tree trunk. A series of soft ripping noises and crackles awoke him from a long and dreamless sleep, and then the main trunk shuddered as if something inside it had suddenly changed position.

He was on his feet and out from under the periphery of Tree in one fluid movement, surprising even himself at the speed with which he had moved. But Tree seemed just the same, nothing else happened, except for one of the lower branches bending down, offering him his morning meal.

Jed was thinking about going out to the lava field to see if he could learn a little more about the strange compound which made up the great rolling billows of soft foam like rock, when he got a message from Tree.

To be more exact, he got a hazy picture of himself putting the Shard crystal into a hole in the main trunk, and then running away up to the top of the first big slopes at the edge of the sand plain.

He approached the tree cautiously, walking around the trunk looking for the opening, but there was no sign of a break in the smooth brown green structure, much less a cavity. Returning to the Shard, he picked it up with great care and waited for the next 'instruction', hoping one would be forthcoming.

The same ripping noise which had accompanied the opening of his 'birth chamber' so long ago, made him jump involuntarily. A long vertical split opened before him, and he could see deep within the main trunk.

A vertical oval chamber with a flat base invited him to place the Shard crystal within it, and as his head and shoulders brushed against the sides of the opening, he noticed they felt fibrous, soft, and warm.

The air within the chamber had a warm, musty, spicy smell, which he found not unpleasant, although totally alien to anything he had ever experienced before. He paused for a moment to breathe in several lungs full of the heady atmosphere of the chamber, finding it had a soothing and calming effect on the tension he just realized he was feeling.

As he lowered the Shard onto the flat base of the chamber, a ring of fibrous looking material exuded itself upwards to grip the base of the Shard firmly but gently, and then he heard the rustle of the outer layer of the trunk as it began to close off the cavity. A quick exit was called for, lest he be incorporated into whatever Tree was about to do.

Within a few moments, the trunk was sealed up tight as though it had never opened, and then he remembered the picture of him running away from Tree, and hastily took to his heels for the distant sand slope.

Jed sat down on top of the sand ridge from which he had seen the flower stalk the previous day, and wondered if the Shard and the bulbous lump on the end of the tall stalk were somehow linked in an alien marriage of pollination, but he could not see how a lump of mineral could combine with an organic material to produce further life, even if it were in the form of seeds.

By mid morning, nothing much had happened, and Jed began to wonder if he had interpreted the message correctly.

A slight movement of the stalk caught his eye, and he put his full attention on it as the pod and stalk began to lower slowly but surely downwards, until both were hidden by the copious foliage which crowned the top of the massive tree.

As the midday sun reached its highest point in the hard blue sky, Jed sensed an electric feeling in the air, and knew something momentous was about to happen.

There was slight movement in the top of the tree and Jed fixed his attention on it, but he was not expecting what happened next.

The huge seed pod and the supporting stalk shot skywards at an astonishing rate, accelerating all the time until it was a good fifty metres high above the tree's canopy. As it went up, the stalk thinned down until it was a mere shadow of its former self, and then there was a dull thump as the seed pod detached itself and soared ever upwards.

Jed watched in amazement as the pod dwindled into a tiny speck high above, and then it burst silently into a cloud of what looked like mist. The cloud rapidly expanded in every direction until it had thinned out so much that he was not sure if it was still there or not.

When the concussion wave hit him, it rattled every bone in his body and blurred his vision. Now he knew why Tree wanted him to leave the immediate area.

The magnificent stalk which had so proudly held the seed pod aloft was now in tatters, like so many crumpled dirty ribbons, scattered about among the upper canopy.

Even as he watched in shocked amazement, Tree began slowly pulling in the shattered remains of the stalk, to no doubt recycle the material into something else Tree might need, as nothing was wasted in such a harsh environment.

A few moments later, and Tree looked none the worse for the spore dispersal exercise, and Jed thought it safe to return to its welcome shade for a while.

Beside the huge trunk lay the Shard, now in its black form with all its energy spent, but still a thing of great beauty. He picked it up and carried it away some fifty metres from Tree, somehow knowing it was of no further use, but a pleasant thing to look at just the same.

Over the time he had been with Tree, Jed had quartered the area within his reach for things of interest, and had now exhausted what few anomalies the planet had to offer, although he never did fully resolve how the foamed lava was formed, or why.

It was time again to see if Tree would help him travel a bit further afield, and to this end he tried once more to communicate his wishes to the huge growth, whom he considered to be his benefactor, of sorts. Jed had a sneaky feeling that he was somehow responsible for Tree's existence in the first place, and without his aid, Tree would have been unable to scatter its spores across the plain.

But then again, Tree had supplied him with a very efficient body well suited to this strange planet, and kept him in food, so they were equal in a sense. Tree still held the ace card, insofar that it controlled the food supply, and that, of necessity, restricted Jed's movements.

That evening he leaned against the mighty trunk, and ran mental image pictures in his mind of him going a great distance to see what the large dark object just below the horizon was. The difficult part was conveying the concept of a regular food supply, and a means of carrying it.

Tree did not respond in any way he could detect, but then it never did, so he just hoped that something would materialize from his efforts. Two days later it did.

Jed had just consumed his morning meal and was wondering what to do next, when he noticed a large branch suddenly begin to move. It was a slow process, but gradually it lowered itself so that it was just level with his head.

On the end of the branch was a large dark green pear shaped object, dangling on a stalk which did not look strong enough to have born its weight.

As it did not look anything like his normal food supply, Jed wondered if it might be in response to his request to travel further afield, but if it was some kind of food it would only last a few days at most, so it looked as if he still had a distance restriction.

As he approached the pear shaped creation there was a faint 'snap', and he had to lunge forward to catch it before it hit the ground. But what was it? It was certainly very heavy and solid, but apart from a groove running around its middle and a strange cruciform pattern on the top where the stalk had broken off, it was featureless.

As for biting into it, he doubted if his teeth would be able to tackle the very tough looking outer skin which had a hard, almost metallic feel to it.

Jed sat down against the trunk of his provider, cradling the gift on his lap and trying to formulate a picture which asked 'what do I do with it?' He closed his eyes so as to concentrate, and a vague and hazy picture of the 'pear' sitting on the ground formed briefly, and then was gone.

Jed could not see what the point of placing it on the ground was, but walked out just beyond the area shaded by Tree to see what would happen when he did. Placing the 'pear' on the sandy ground, he stood back and waited.

A few moments later the top half split around the annular groove and rose up about ten centimetres. From the area of the groove, a mass of fine hairs sprang out and seemed to be vibrating or shimmering, although it was difficult to see exactly what they were doing as they were so fine.

Jed reached forward and tried to lift the 'pear', but it seemed to be rooted to the ground, which he thought a bit odd, as the ground was only sand. He sat down to watch what would happen next, if anything.

Jed was getting a little impatient because nothing of any consequence had happened for some time, and he did not see much point in watching the 'pear' thing any longer.

He was just about to get up when the fringe of hairs around its middle retracted back inside, the top lowered to its former position and the cruciform pattern on the top opened out and folded down like the petals of a flower in full bloom.

Perched on top of the 'pear' was a food plum, just like the one Tree produced for his meals. Jed was almost too astonished to move, but he did eventually, and reached out to pick up the yellow food globe. He inspected it closely, it looked the same, the colour and weight were about right, and it had the same delicious heady aroma he looked forward to twice each day.

Although he had recently eaten, he placed it in his mouth and the skin split, allowing the contents to swill around his taste buds, and then with a gulp, slips down his eager throat.

After he had come to terms, to some degree, with what had happened, Jed picked up his new food dispenser, and noticed there were small indentations in the ground where it had rested. He thought it looked as if the device had sent down roots of some kind, and then withdrawn them on completion of its action.

As he turned to go back and sit down against the trunk again, he noticed several long thin strands hanging down from a nearby branch. One by one they fell to the ground, and then he realized Tree had produced them to make a sling or holding net for the food dispenser.

He stopped in mid stride. That idea had come clearly to his mind, the picture was bright and clear, and not of his own making. Tree had improved its communication ability considerably.

Jed gathered up the fine tendrils Tree had kindly produced, and sat down against the mighty trunk to make himself a bag-like net in which to carry the food dispenser. The strands were fine, pliable, and very strong, being of the same colour as the branch they had come from. Having completed the net, he wove a belt which he could put around his waist and attach the net to, so leaving both hands free when travelling, which he somehow felt might be necessary.

How the dispenser worked took most of the night to fathom out, but he arrived at what he thought might be a possible explanation. The device put down roots into the ground, and by some means managed to extract whatever minerals and other materials it needed.

The fringe of fine hairs, he decided, somehow absorbed atmospheric water vapour, oxygen, and carbon dioxide, the internal mechanism of the dispenser breaking these down to form the building blocks of the more complex molecules necessary to construct the fabric of the food plum.

How the whole thing was powered remained a mystery, and he never did solve that.

Now that he had a food supply, and by default, permission to go on his travels, Jed felt sorry in a way that he was leaving Tree to its own devices. It had been company of a sort, and he felt strangely guilty putting his own desires first, and not considering what Tree wanted. But then again, he mused, if Tree did not want him to leave, he would not have got his food generator, or the bag to put it in.

Jed finally decided that next morning he would leave, but before doing so would try and communicate to Tree that he would return one day to see how the mammoth growth was getting on, and if it needed another helping hand with the pollination exercise.

Early the following morning, as the sun splashed the horizon with its usual of blaze of coloured streamers, Jed was awake and ready for his first meal of the day, which Tree obligingly provided. Having satisfied his need for sustenance, he picked up his bag containing the food producer, and approached the giant trunk again.

It was not easy trying to construct pictures to show his intent, but he did his best, finishing with him coming back to see Tree in the future. He could discern no response to his communication attempts, so he tied the belt with its bag around his waist, gave the mighty trunk a firm slap in farewell, and walked away.

From his earlier excursions, he knew roughly the direction he should travel to reach the dark construction below the horizon, and having gone a couple of hundred metres from Tree, turned and gave it a wave.

One of the higher branches seemed to dip in response, but it might have been Tree rearranging itself for some other purpose. He gave himself the benefit of the doubt as to what had really happened, and felt all the sorrier for leaving.

By midmorning he had reached the edge of the plain on which Tree grew, and the landscape changed to the rolling mounds of sand and gravel once more. The undulating terrain slowed his progress more than he would have liked, but with his new found strength, he seemed to tire hardly at all compared to his old body, which he had almost forgotten about.

A particularly high bank of gravel formed the end of the undulating terrain, and before him stretched a series of gently rounded low hills, the surface of which was the never ending sand and gravel, but this time the gravel predominated, and was a little larger than before.

Four:
The Dome

IN THE FAR distance, something caught his eye. It was rounded, but not quite like the low hills which seemed to reach to the horizon, and it was darker in colour. He knew it could not be the dark construction he had seen on his earlier travels as it was not large enough.

Jed set off with renewed vigour, the sharp crunch of his footfalls being the only sound, apart from the air rushing in and out of his lungs as he increased his pace still further.

By evening, he had covered three quarters of the distance to the dome shaped object, and the details were now much clearer. It was large by any standard, and seemed to be on a flattened area all of its own, almost as if a hill top had been cut away to give it a platform on which to sit. He was now totally convinced that it had been constructed.

He was tempted to travel on during the hours of darkness, but common sense prevailed, and he settled down for the night in a convenient depression where the gravel was smaller and a little less sharp.

Taking the food pod, as he had christened it, out of the net bag, Jed pressed it down firmly on the ground next to him, giving it a little wriggle for good measure.

The aromatic plums were all very well, but he fancied something different for a change, a good chunk of cooked meat would go down very nicely he thought, but perhaps his new body would be unable to cope with such fare.

The pod ran through its routine while Jed patiently waited for the top to open, which it eventually did. Picking up the plum, he placed it in his mouth and waited for the skin to split, and hit his taste buds with its aromatic contents.

Nothing happened, so he bit down hard to help it along, and nearly choked at the result.

There was no soft scented goo to slip deliciously down his throat, but a firm chewy meat flavoured concoction which rolled around his mouth, refusing to be swallowed until it had been ground down to a fine pulp.

'Good God. The bloody thing can read my thoughts.' Jed was more surprised and a little more frightened than he would have liked to admit. After the initial shock, he continued to chew on his mouthful of meat flavoured fibre, and eventually managed to swallow it, deciding he would be very careful what he thought about next time he set the pod up to produce his meal.

The fear content of his surprise dissipated as he realized the pod did not have to be a 'thinking being' in order to carry out his wishes; it could be programmed to duplicate what was desired. But then, what picked up his thoughts? He was back where he had started.

Tree had never produced anything other than the aromatic flavoured food plums, so perhaps he had not recalled any of his old foods when he was with Tree. He could not be sure.

'Perhaps it was Tree's little joke. Oh God, now I'm imbuing Tree with a sense of humour!' He gave up, and settled down for a good nights sleep, but it did not come for a while.

It was a very careful Jed who placed the food pod down next morning, constraining his thoughts to the type of food plum Tree had always supplied, and was rewarded with the 'standard' food he had become used to. He decided to put food experiments to one side for the time being.

The rising sun lit up the distant building in a brilliant flash of fire, making it stand out from its surroundings very clearly like a flaming torch, but the shape quickly changed, verifying Jed's notion that it was a domed structure.

Gathering up his net bag, Jed broke into a jog up the first slope of many he was to face before reaching the distant domed structure which intrigued him so much.

In one of the shallow valleys he came across another collection of petrified branches, this time with a large section of main trunk, although it was not as large as Tree used to support its massive canopy.

'Could there have been a forest of trees at one time?' He wondered what the planet would have looked like, covered in a green mantle instead of the barren sand and gravel which seemed to prevail at the present moment.

The remains were very heavy, and must have been converted to stone in the very distant past, so how had Tree's seed managed to survive so long? As usual, each question spawned yet more questions, instead of answers, so he decided to just accept what he saw, bearing in mind that alien and unusual things happen on alien worlds.

Slowly but surely, the domed structure grew bigger each time Jed reached the top of the next hill in the long succession of rolling mounds of gravel, until he was on the top of the last one, and looking down on the dome.

It was far bigger than he had thought, some five to six hundred metres in diameter but only about twenty high. He approached the structure with the usual amount of caution afforded to things he did not understand, and was soon within touching distance of the walls.

They seemed to be made of some seamless dark grey, or almost black material, shot through with tiny flecks of sparkling light as though the surface was almost transparent.

Jed reached out to touch the surface of the wall and was surprised to feel a slick silky smoothness, akin to that of glass with an invisible layer of some lubricant on it.

He had never come across anything like it before, and stood there for some minutes, gently stroking the alien surface in deep fascination. He then noticed he was beginning to feel sleepy, and quickly took his hand away from the glistening surface, realizing that the wall probably had some built in system for deterring unwanted inquisitive creatures like him.

Jed began to walk around the massive structure to find an entrance, which he felt sure must exist somewhere, although it might be hidden or disguised in some way.

When he had circumnavigated the dome at least once, and what he thought was well on the way to a second circuit, he found the entrance. A three metre square recess, six metres deep, was set in the curved wall.

Jed walked in warily, looking for anything unusual, but it was just what it looked like, a featureless alcove. He could see no doorway or other means of entry, and was about to return to the outside world when he noticed a small section of wall which seemed to glow from within.

Not knowing exactly why, he reached up and placed his hand on it, and the glow faded. As he took his hand away, the back section of the alcove moved back a little and then slid silently to one side, revealing a further cavity beyond.

The decision as to whether he should enter the newly exposed recess was taken out of his hands when the whole area glowed with a pale light. He could not see where it was coming from; it just seemed to fill the space with a soft radiance. He felt that whoever activated the entrance was intended to go in, so he did.

The wall slid back cutting off the outside world, and Jed felt a surge of panic. Suppose he could not get out again?

It was too late now; he was held captive in an alien structure, and no operating manual.

Suddenly the floor fell from under him with a sickening lurch, and Jed almost got the sensation of free fall. By the time he had got his balance back, his stomach tried to slide down to his knees as the lift slowed and came to a stop.

The back section of the lift slid to one side, and he was looking out onto a gallery which ran around the inside of the dome. Apart from the unexpected and unpleasant sensation of the lift, no harm had come to him, so he stepped out onto the gallery, and the lift door quietly slid to behind him.

The air had a touch of ozone in it, along with the other odours associated with heavy electrical discharge, so his first thought was that the dome might be a generator of some kind. It took a few moments for Jed's eyes to get used to the low level of light within the dome chamber, and when they did, he was in for another shock. He had gone up to the protecting balustrade at the edge of the gallery to look at what he first thought was a massive column of disks, and then, as his eyes managed to focus on them, realized that they were revolving at high speed.

The highest disk rotated between a series of large bulbous shapes spaced evenly around its periphery, and possibly these were the take off points for the power being generated.

Jed estimated that the top disk was at least fifty metres in diameter and four to five metres thick. Each disk in the descending column was a little larger in diameter than the one above it, forming a pyramid of disks disappearing below the level of the gallery into a huge hole which looked as if it went right down to the very core of the planet.

It was the sheer size of the machinery which astounded him, and the fact that it was almost silent, there being only the faintest high pitched whirring sound, and that was only just audible.

The spinning disks pulled the air around with them, causing a gentle draft in the dome which Jed found refreshing; being the first time since landing on the planet he had felt a constant air flow.

He expected to see huge power cables, control consoles and the like, if this was indeed an electrical generator, but the dome was devoid of such things, and if they existed, were well hidden from sight.

Jed returned to the point where he thought he had entered the dome, but there was no sign of the lift doorway, or any other features.

The walls and the gallery floor were seamlessly joined as if the whole colossal edifice had been cast in one piece.

The usual flash of panic swept through him as it did when he felt restricted or trapped, but then reason took over, and he began a systematic search for the elusive lift.

Jed remembered he could sometimes see things using his peripheral vision, when viewing something straight on revealed nothing. Pacing up and down and not looking directly at the wall was not quite as easy as he had thought, but persistence paid off in the end as he caught a glimpse of two circular sections of wall which seemed to have a little extra light of their own.

Having located them, it was easy to pick them out again, and he wondered what light frequency the eyes of the dome builders worked at, it certainly differed from his. Or maybe the strange light within the dome had a masking effect.

Two round patches on the wall, one above the other, seemed to be the controls for something, he hoped it was the lift, and he assumed he had a choice of going up or down. Jed put his hand on the lower patch and the wall obligingly opened, inviting him into the unknown.

This time he was ready for the downwards surge, but it still caught him off balance, and went on for a lot longer. His knees almost bent as the lift decelerated and came to a stop. The wall slid back, and he was in the lower most level of the power generator.

This chamber was much larger than the one above, and the whole space, apart from a very narrow gallery running around the wall, was filled by the huge column of disks.

To save a long search later, Jed took off his net bag and left it as a marker for locating the lift, and then went over to the balustrade to see if he could make sense of the giant column of disks.

All but the highest disk seemed to be motionless, and that was only just moving. He estimated the lowest disk to be in the order of four hundred metres across, and ten metres thick, but as it disappeared below the gallery floor, its true thickness was hidden from view.

The material from which the lower most disk was made differed from all the others, and he found it difficult to focus his eyes on the shimmering surface. It reminded him of thin translucent smoke, and yet, when he turned his head to one side, it looked solid enough.

Jed leaned on the balustrade deep in thought.

'If the disks in the top of the dome were turning, and the highest one here was moving, even though very slightly, then they all should be in motion, to some degree,' he reasoned, 'so let's see.' He went back to the net bag, and finding an untidy strand sticking out from the side, chewed off a small piece.

Careful not to touch the giant disk, he leaned over the balustrade and gently lowered the fragment to its surface, half expecting it to drift down through the ghostly substance.

Using the end of one toe as a marker, Jed patiently stood there, daring the fragment of his net bag to move. It was some time later before he could be certain that the base disk was actually moving, but the movement was infinitesimal, and only just observable. Without his piece of net bag, he would never have known for sure.

He then studied the other disks in the column a little more closely, and found that they all moved, but very slowly, each disk rotating a little faster than the one below.

'That's why I didn't see the movement in the first place,' he thought, 'the difference in rotation between each one is so small as to be hardly noticeable.'

Bit by bit, the alien construction revealed its secrets as Jed applied his logic and scientific knowledge. To him, the whole mighty column of disks represented a gear box, each disk driving the one above a little faster, until the top one in the dome above acquired the necessary rotational velocity to generate what he assumed to be electricity.

The main disk at the bottom of the column proved a little more difficult to rationalize as it was turning so slowly, and he could think of nothing which would do that naturally.

The strange material of the driving disk must contain the answer to how it was driven, he concluded, and then his only workable theory fell into place.

The bottom disk did not move, it was locked in position by some external force, and the planet moved, or rotated, around it, so causing the other disks to rotate. The only thing he could think of which rotated so slowly was the planet itself. Therefore the sun around which it circled must be the holding force, and that somehow held the driving disk locked in the same direction, while the planet slowly turned around it.

Jed was not totally satisfied with his explanation, but it was the best he could do without a lot of test equipment, which he was sadly lacking.

While he was down in the basement, so to speak, he thought it prudent to complete his walk around the gallery, just to make sure there were no other clues which might increase his knowledge of the alien constructors.

By the time he had returned to his net bag, marking the lift portal, he was none the wiser. There were no control panels or other devices decorating the glass smooth walls of the chamber, and he thought it about time he returned to the world above.

He entered the lift and placed his hand on the upper of the two faintly illuminated patches on the wall, preparing for the rapid up surge, but it was a little more than he was expecting and his knees buckled under the acceleration.

'What the hell sort of people where they?' he mused, as the lift reached the top of its shaft and suddenly stopped, causing him to feel as if he were floating for a brief moment.

The side of the lift cavity quietly slid open, and he was out in the bright sunlight once more, except that the sun was now near the horizon, and that made him realize just how low the light level was within the dome.

He decided to stay near the dome for the night, as the sun would soon plunge his world into darkness, and he needed the rising sun to set his bearings by for the next part of his journey. Having found the dome, he felt his main quest could well turn out to be another alien building, somewhere below the horizon line.

A slightly uneasy and brief thought about an expensive and rare fruit from his home world, and the food pod obliged, making a most pleasant end to his day of exploration.

The blazing sun had climbed half way up the sky when Jed reached the last of the low hills he had been climbing up and down all morning. Before him stretched a boring flat plain of the ubiquitous sand and gravel mix, except this time there were odd groups of finger like dark rocks sticking up in little clumps to break the monotony.

Jed had passed several clumps, without paying them much heed, when the symmetry of one group attracted his attention. They were spaced just a little too evenly for the casual dispersion of nature, even on this planet.

Close up, the columns of rock appeared more like constructed pillars than a natural mineral deposit, except the surface looked as if it had been liquefied and dribbled downwards, creating an uneven rippled effect. Some parts were shot through with a rainbow of scintillating colours, like oil on water, adding to the unnatural effect.

At first, Jed thought the pillars had supported something, a building maybe, but there were no traces of anything else other than the rocky stumps, and he could envisage no useful purpose for them on their own.

Jed happened to look down at the gravel, and found it different to that which he had seen before. On the terrain he had travelled across so far, the gravel had always been sharp, as if it had been recently crushed down from larger stones, but here, it was rounded, rather like beach pebbles, and that could only mean one thing, it had been worn round by being tumbled around in water.

Had there been a sea here? Or a large river? If there had, he reasoned it must have been a very long time ago, as the planet seemed almost devoid of free water now with only a small amount held in the atmosphere, and that was insufficient to precipitate rain, as far as he knew.

Someone or something, in the dim and distant past had taken a dislike to the pillars and what they supported, and had subjected them to a heat so intense that it vaporized whatever was on top, and melted the stonework, making it run like thick treacle. He hoped they were not still around.

Jed marched on, leaving the stricken pillars behind and wondering if they predated the dome, which was constructed from a different material and was in pristine condition.

The gravel plain eventually gave way to an area where there had been a vast up thrust of rocks from below, making the going very difficult, and that too had occurred in the distant past, as the surface of the rocks had been worn smooth by sand abrasion. The sand now filled the gaps between most of them, with the occasional ridge standing proudly bare for Jed to climb over.

It was while he sat on a ridge resting, and cursing his luck for having such a barrier to surmount, that he realized for the rocks to have been sandblasted, there must have been a considerable wind to drive the sand.

So where was the wind now? He had never known a place to be so devoid of air movement, not even a gentle breeze as the planet's surface warmed and cooled each day.

At last, and with a sigh of relief, he scrambled down the last ridge in the rock field and was back on sand. Soft, smooth, and fortunately compacted, so his feet only left faint impressions as he increased his pace to make up for lost time.

In the distance he could see what looked like another ridge of rock, but it was only a short one, and could be easily circumnavigated. As he drew near to the ridge, he realized it was not just random rock, but a constructed wall of some kind, and of a similar type of material as that of the dome.

As Jed approached what he thought was a straight section wall, it became apparent that it was a circular enclosure, about one hundred metres across and two metres high, so he was unable to see what it enclosed, if anything.

The seamless wall was a deep slate grey, with none of the little flecks of light sparkling within it like the material of the dome, but Jed felt the two were somehow related.

Unable to peer over the rim, he tried to grip the top and heave himself up. The next moment he was flat on his back, spitting out a mouthful of sand and too surprised to add the usual expletive to his thoughts.

Having dusted himself off, he ran his hand over the smooth surface of the wall and got the sensation that there was an outer invisible layer, which when touched, slid over the main body of the construction, making the whole thing frictionless.

Determined to see what was on the other side, Jed began to laboriously scrape sand into a pile next to the wall, tamping it down firmly so that it would take his not inconsiderable weight without collapsing.

As he put his foot on the pile, the sand in contact with the wall slid away, as if it were loath to be in contact with the slippery surface, and the step began to collapse.

Jed increased the width of his step, and tried again. This time he was able to peer over the wall, and look down onto a mirror, one hundred metres across. The surface was flawless, reflecting the hard blue sky above and a perfect mirror image of the wall's inner surface, making the wall look twice as deep as it really was.

He expected to see something on the mirror's surface, even if it were only a few grains of sand, but there was nothing to mar the pristine reflection of the sky, giving him the sensation that his world had turned upside down.

Jed could not understand how the mirror remained free from the usual detritus which he would have expected to see on its surface, so he wanted to see what happened to anything introduced to the enclosure.

He had to walk some way before he found a piece of gravel large enough for his experiment, and having collected a good handful, returned to the walled enclosure intent on solving the mystery.

He dropped the first piece onto the mirror, but close to the wall. The multiple reflections distorted what happened, but it seemed to just disappear.

The next piece of gravel was thrown a little further out, and that was when he realized it was not a solid mirror at all. The small stone hit the surface, and a tiny ring of molten mirror rippled out for a short distance before the treacle like material damped the motion out, and the piece of gravel seemed to dissolve before his eyes, the mirror returning to its former condition of a perfect reflection of the sky above.

Several more pieces of gravel followed, until he had run out of missiles, and they all seemed to dissolve in the silver looking liquid, leaving no trace of their former selves.

'I wonder what would happen to organic matter.' Jed thought, and taking his food pod out of its bag, he placed it firmly on the sandy ground, and waited.

When the food plum appeared after the prescribed time, he carefully climbed once more onto his sand step, and tossed the plum into the mirror pool.

A small, quickly fading viscous ripple was accompanied by a puff of water vapour, which instantly dispersed in the arid atmosphere, and the silver pool was still once more.

Jed wondered if he would have nightmares about falling into the all dissolving pool, and he was right.

As fascinating as the pool was, he knew he would learn little more by randomly tossing debris into it, so he left the pool behind and continued his journey, the alien nature of the pool's mechanism foremost in his mind as he trudged on towards the horizon.

It was almost sunset when he finally figured out what the pool was all about. He thought of it as a giant cement or materials mixer, only it converted everything put in it to a set formula, decreed by whatever magical potion was placed in the pool to begin with.

Virtually anything added to the pool thereafter was transformed into the 'mirror liquid', and that he supposed was used to construct the seamless buildings, something causing the liquid to set solid at a predetermined stage.

'But how do you transport something which dissolves everything it touches?' he asked himself, and then remembered the strange invisible slippery skin which covered the pool's walls.

The light was beginning to fade a little, so when he found a shallow dip in the ground he stopped for the night, and set up the food pod.

Also the terrain was changing yet again. It looked as if some huge underground force had been unleashed and puckered the land mass up into a series of frozen waves, and then tilted one end of them up a few degrees. It looked easy enough to traverse, but he thought it was better to do so in full daylight.

That night he dreamt of the dome and its whirling disks, and then of the silver pool. He watched in horror as his body slowly and painlessly dissolved in the silver liquid, and he became at one with its contents, waiting to be used for some bizarre construction which no one could decide on.

Setting his direction from the rising sun, Jed set off for the first of the giant ripples in the land ahead, none too pleased at the thought of more climbing, but there seemed no easy way around the petrified waves of once molten rock.

The journey across the rippled landscape was boring, and his mind began to wander onto other things. He had not urinated since taking on his new body, as he was not equipped with the means to do so, and only twice had he felt the need to evacuate what he thought were his bowels, squatting down and producing a small hard pellet from between his legs. He continued to be amazed at the efficiency of his body, and its meagre water needs.

Deep in thought and automatically striding on, Jed had not noticed the end of the giant land ripples until he was on the last down slope. Ahead of him a dark structure squatted ominously on the plain, which stretched on to the hazy horizon. As he drew nearer and details became clearer, it lost its menacing look, transforming into a square block with a hole in the middle.

Standing ten metres high and wide, and only two metres thick, it looked as if someone had begun something, and then forgotten what it was they were trying to construct. The hole in the middle was like a doorway, but there was no door, just a view of the plain ahead.

Jed walked around it, looking for a clue as to what it was for, and not finding a utilitarian use for it, decided it must be a monument of some kind, and no doubt of great significance to the builders.

He stood looking at the view beyond the opening, and then, not knowing quite why, walked in. As he reached midway through the arch, the flat seemingly endless plain ahead of him disappeared, and he was in total darkness.

As he was already moving forward quite quickly, he was unable to prevent himself from taking the next step, and suddenly it was light again. The plain ahead looked different, low hills now formed the horizon, and they were only a few kilometres away.

Jed stood there, transfixed, suddenly realizing what had happened to him. He had been transported a considerable distance by walking through an archway, and looking back through the opening, could only see a flat featureless plain right up to the horizon.

He walked slowly around the arch, looking for anything he could have missed on the other one, something which might trigger its operation. As with the first arch, there was nothing but the same smooth dark material, similar to that which the dome was made from.

'What if I walk through this one, in the same direction?' No sooner had he formulated the thought, and his feet propelled him forward of their own volition. Again the darkness, and a new scene as he emerged into daylight.

Before him was an edifice, dark, mysterious and very big. He was facing one corner of the building, and it stretched off on each side for as far as he could see. It looked only a few metres high, with a flat top that stretched off into infinity, but he realized that distance can distort apparent size.

He had reached his goal, it was a mere half kilometre away, yet in a strange way he was reluctant to approach it any further in case the whole thing was a mirage, and his arduous journey had been for nothing.

A shudder ran through his body, and Jed put his strange feelings down to the fact that he had been shot halfway around the planet in a device which he knew could not exist, let alone do what it did.

With a final shrug of his shoulders, Jed strode off towards the dark monolith before him, knowing full well his fears were really unfounded.

It took a lot longer than expected to actually reach the mammoth building, and he was beginning to think there was some sort of defence system, which only gave the illusion of the building being near, or somehow created more ground for him to travel over as he went long.

The building seemed to be constructed from the same material as the dome, with little flecks of light twinkling away just below the surface, and making the actual surface very hard to focus on. There was no sign of an entrance or any other features, just the plain dark walls reaching up for fifteen metres, and stretching out on each side for ever.

As with the dome, he thought there must be an access point somewhere, and began the long walk to find it.

By evening, the featureless wall remained featureless, no sign of a doorway or even a hint that one might exist. With one final look in both directions in case he had missed anything, Jed stopped for the night. The food pod did its thing, producing his meal faithfully, and he then settled down to watch the sinking sun splash the horizon in a multitude of coloured fire streaks, a sight he always enjoyed.

Sleep was long in coming, and he lay there thinking over the various events which had befallen him since the escape pod had crashed so long ago, and the utter hopelessness he had felt before he had encountered Tree.

Things had been looking up ever since, and he felt optimistic for the future, especially now that he had found the building he had seen in his 'free' earlier travels.

Somehow he felt the building was important to him, and a new cycle of life was about to begin.

The sun arose before Jed next morning, its bright light splashing across his eyes and nudging him from an eventual long and deep sleep.

Maybe he had been too tired to notice it last night, or perhaps it was the low angle of the rising sun, but straight in front of him was the elusive doorway to the building.

The faint outline of the square opening was only just visible, more of a hint of something rather than a definite shape. Jed staggered to his feet and shakily walked over to the wall, determined not to lose the entrance now that he had found it.

Scraping two lines of sand into little ridges, each marking the extremity of the ghostly pattern on the wall, he returned to where he had left the net bag, it was time for sustenance.

The food pod had excelled itself this morning, producing an exceptionally fine flavoured plum, and for the first time Jed thought he would like another one. Not knowing if it would produce another in such quick succession, he lifted the pod up and placed it down again in the cold sand.

Pod obediently went through its routine, and while Jed rolled the contents of the plum around in his mouth to get the maximum satisfaction from the delicious pulp, he wondered if he could produce a small stock of plums in case he had difficulty in exiting the building.

While Jed rearranged the knots on the top half of the net bag, making the holes small enough to retain the plums, the food pod was put into production, being lifted and replaced on the sand several times.

When the pod had produced enough plums to keep him going for the next few days, Jed found the pod was quite hot, and left it to cool down as the plums would be placed on top of the pod, and they might deteriorate from the heat.

With the food pod safely back in its bag, and the plums carefully arranged around the top, Jed went to inspect the entrance.

If he had not made the sand markers, he would have missed the pattern on the wall, for the sun had climbed a little higher in the sky and the outline of the entrance had all but disappeared.

He tried to trace the outline of the opening by running his hand over the silk smooth surface, starting from just above the left-hand marker. As his hand wandered over to the right a little, it suddenly found no resistance and he nearly fell forward into the cavity behind the illusion of a solid wall.

He could still see the hazy spectre of his hand and half an arm as he moved it about in apparent solid stone.

'So how many other entrances have I missed on my way here?' he mused, remembering the long non productive walk of yesterday, 'and why such an odd way of hiding the entrance when they could have used something like the lift doors in the dome?'

It seemed the dome, pool, arches, and constructors of the edifice, were one and the same, as the same type of material had been used for all four, except the pool had an extra skin of something indefinable.

Procrastination was something Jed did not indulge in, usually, but he now paced up and down outside the entrance to the edifice, occasionally thrusting his hand into the illusion of a solid wall, while he considered if he really wanted to commit himself to something he could not comprehend, let alone understand.

Not too sure whether it was his decision, or if something else had given him a mental nudge, he turned, faced the apparently solid wall, and boldly walked into his future.

Once he had passed through the illusion, he turned and looked back to see if the plain was still there. It was, though it appeared a little hazy now, as if it was being viewed through glass over which water was trickling.

Just to be sure he was not trapped, Jed walked back through the phantom wall and onto the crunchy sand of the plain.

Having satisfied himself that he could return to the outside world if he chose, he returned to the cavity behind the illusionary wall and the passageway which led into the building.

As he walked along, the muffled pad pad of his footfalls echoed back softly from the walls, giving the illusion that he was being followed, but he sensed he was alone.

The passage had the same quality of light as had the dome, it just seemed to be there, softly flooding the whole area, but without a specific source point.

Fifty metres in, the passageway ended in a solid wall. Jed ran is hands over it, looking for whatever mechanism the constructors had thought fit to use as an opening device, but found nothing which would operate the barrier.

He had the uncanny sensation that he was being scrutinized by something, as a warm sensation washed over him. Jed stepped back from the blanking wall as it silently slid to one side, revealing another cavity beyond.

This was reminiscent of the lifts he had used in the dome, and it was with some trepidation that he stepped into the square chamber, preparing himself for the expected sudden drop which always caught him unawares.

Jed waited for the lift to move, but nothing happened. He was about to look for some means of returning to the passage when the back wall of the cavity slid sideways, and he looked out into the largest enclosed space he had ever seen.

Five:
The Collection

As Jed stepped out into the seemingly infinite chamber, the lift exit slid to behind him, leaving no trace of ever having existed. The panic feeling went as quickly as it had come, he was getting used to the idea that doors always hid themselves, although he could see no reason why they should.

The hall stretched out before him, and apart from the wall behind him, seemed to have no limit, fading out into the hazy distance in all directions. The same soft light pervaded all, casting no shadows from the countless thousands of box-like objects which lay in evenly spaced neat rows.

He went up to the nearest wraith like object, which looked like a hardly visible transparent plastic block mounted on a waist high plinth of the same material as the rest of the building. But the block, when he tried to touch it, had no temperature, and returned no tactile sensation whatever.

It was hard to focus his eyes on its surface, not from insufficient light, but because the surface did not seem to be there when he looked directly at it.

This was quite different to all the other anomalies he had found on the planet, and he backed away, not liking the strange sensation he received when trying to touch the block.

When concentrating his attention on a block, he noticed that those around it had a very slight shimmer to their outlines, and that gave him the clue as to what they were.

He remembered a scientific paper long ago on the theory of force fields, how they could be generated, and some of their possible uses, not that anyone had actually made one.

If force fields really existed, then these were they, but according to theory, they existed entirely independent of time and space, and the rest of the physical world.

Although he felt uneasy about the blocks in some inexplicable way, he knew he would have to overcome his feelings if he were to understand the purpose of the vast complex, and there was a burning desire to do that.

Jed approached one of the blocks again, and peered into its almost non existent surface. Resting on the bottom of the transparent cuboid was a tiny plant, its bright green floret of leaflets spread out in perfect symmetry around a short central stem on which the next set of leaflets were just ready to burst out from their budding stage.

It looked so fresh and alive, and yet it was trapped in space and time, in permanent suspended animation and unrelated to anything else in the physical universe. If the theories were correct.

He moved on to the next exhibit, where another plant differing only slightly from the first one by the size and colour of its leaves, sat in a state of stasis, yet looking as if it had only just sprouted its inner most set of leaflets and was getting ready to produce the next set.

As he wandered down the long line of exhibits, each one differing in some subtle way from its predecessor, the idea formed in his mind that this was a repository of some kind, a place where a sample of every permutation of a species was held for some future reference.

In the distance, and over to one side, he could see some larger transparent blocks, and hurried over to them. They contained a variety of tree ferns, some resembling those he had seen as fossils in a museum, and others which had mutated into bizarre forms, necessary no doubt to suit their particular environments, wherever they were.

Jed stopped his frantic rushing from one display to another, and looked around, trying to take in the whole scene.

Each plant type seemed to begin with its most basic form, and as he went down the infinite line of exhibits, these subtlety changed to cover every possible permutation that a plant could develop to suit just about every imaginable environment, and some he found hard to envisage.

Jed moved some distance across the hall to see what other species of plants had been collected, and stopped at a brown withered specimen consisting of a mass of gnarled and twisted tendrils. It looked as if it had been baked under a blazing sun and then trodden on by something exceedingly heavy, with a twisting motion imparted as an after thought.

Going down the line he found many variations on the basic theme, some with flattened tendrils, different colours, soft and spongy, thick, thin, and some which looked almost crystalline by the way light reflected from them.

It was when he looked a little closer at the plinth on which the cubes were mounted that he noticed a subtitle inscription, which differed from plinth to plinth. These were the first symbols he had seen, although they bore no resemblance to any script he had ever come across.

By the time Jed had crossed several hundred species lines, he realized just about everything which could be imagined was here, and he had only covered a small portion of the vast hall which still stretched on into the distance.

He had seen everything from the most basic slime moulds, algae's and lichens, through simple grasses to complex reed like structures and on through the leafed plants to shrubs, trees and a collection of desert plants which beggared description, unless they had been seen.

Each one had its own unique set of symbols as a reference, and he began to wonder what the reference was used for, and who would need to use it.

Jed reasoned that if this level of the complex was devoted to plant life, then there should be other levels which contained other life forms, the animals, insects, and God knows what other creations, garnered from all corners of the universe. He made his way back to the point where he had entered the hall, hoping to find the lift mechanism, but the wall was just one continuous smooth surface, with no sign of an opening or doorway.

It was when he looked upwards to see where the wall joined the ceiling that he saw a line of wedge shapes, the thin ends of which pointed to his right. Jed thought the constructors of the complex would hardly waste their time and effort on so simple a decoration, so assumed that they were indicators of some kind. He followed the line and stood where the wedge points changed direction, and a cavity in the wall obligingly opened for him.

He walked into what he hoped was a lift, and the wall slid to behind him. Halfway up the back wall of the box-like cavity a vertical row of eleven circular light patches softly glowed, the second one down from the top a little brighter than the rest. Jed reasoned that the brighter patch indicated the level at which he now was, and the others belonged to the levels below. He placed his hand on the third patch down.

There was no discernible motion he was aware of, but the wall slid back after a few seconds and he was looking out into the next hall of the collector's mammoth assembly of universal life forms.

The first few exhibits revealed that he was among the insect collection, and he cringed at the thought of meeting some of them in real life. They ranged from the almost microscopic to creatures as large as him, most of which were equipped to deal with anything nature could throw at them.

Two more levels down, and he felt more at home. There were several creatures here not too different from those he had seen in real life, and a couple of animals were easily recognizable as coming from his home world.

It was when he reached the anthropoid section that he became uneasy. Several were familiar, while most were obviously from other worlds, and hideous into the bargain.

Jed crossed over several lines of exhibits to get a species change, when he froze in his tracks.

Staring out from its almost non existent prison was a copy of his former self. There was no doubt in his mind that he had found his own race of people. A shudder ran through him realizing a fellow being had been abducted, to be locked for ever in a timeless existence for another's amusement.

He moved on, trying to forget what he had seen, but knowing it would haunt his dreams for some time to come.

Another section held creatures so large he could not understand how they could support their own weight, let alone move about to feed. He concluded that they must have come from a very low gravity world, but that posed its own problems, as such planets usually failed to hold their atmospheres due to the lack of sufficient mass.

Jed suddenly felt hungry, and withdrew a food plum from his bag. He had no idea of what time of day it was, or how long he had been wandering through the huge collection of life from all over the universe, not that it mattered much.

On the tenth level, things were a little different. There were no plinths with their ghostly blocks, or any sign of life forms, only machinery of a type he had never seen before.

This section of the complex was of finite size, he could at least see two of the walls, although the one facing him was a little indistinct, lost in a haze of distance.

What he thought were conveyors, snaked out from apertures in the side walls of the hall, converging on a series of tables. Above these were several box-like structures which looked as if they could be lowered onto the working surfaces below, but for what purpose he had no idea.

Further on down the great hall, a racking system held huge quantities of canisters, some big enough to have held the largest of the creatures he had seen in the levels above, while some were no bigger than his smallest finger.

As he looked around, he began to formulate a theory which would encompass most, if not all the things he had seen.

Jed supposed the creatures captured from other worlds would be brought into the machinery hall and placed on the work tables. The overhead box like hoods would then descend and create around them the stasis field which would preserve them for ever, and they would then be transported via the conveyors to whichever level their type dictated.

To his way of thinking, the lines of creatures on the levels he had inspected seemed to be complete. So what happened if another 'find' was brought in and there was no space for it within the series of its type? Surely the exhibits would not be shuffled up to make room for it, everything seemed too well laid out for that. He felt he had missed something, failed to understand some little subtlety about the place. Perhaps further exploration would supply the answers.

Jed worked his way on down through the long line of machines, but what most of them did was incomprehensible to him. One thing he did notice was the lack of any symbols, and he thought that a bit odd.

Reaching the far end of the hall, he passed through a portal reminding him of the arch transmitters, which had whisked him across the surface of the planet, was it yesterday?

A brief flash of blackness and a subtle shifting of the very fabric of space caught Jed off guard as he walked through the portal which linked the two halls.

Before him was an immense chamber, the top of which he could not see as it disappeared into the gloom above. In the centre of the floor, a huge column rose upwards like a giant chimney, its sides studded with protuberances of all shapes and sizes, while its base was linked to the encircling walls by a series of twenty metre wide spokes. A vast copper coloured toroid joined each spoke to the central column, and to these were connected cables as thick as his body, hanging down from the side walls in a series of graceful loops, and giving the impression of immense power, but what form it took Jed could not imagine. What he thought were conveyor strips ran between the spokes, and these then disappeared into the side walls of the chamber.

His first thought was that he had located the landing place of the returning ships which had been sent out to collect samples from around the universe, but this did not explain the massive central column which looked more like a huge gun barrel on its end, complete with its unexplained knobs and bumps. It was the sheer scale of things which made him think it was not quite what he though it was, but nothing else came to mind.

Jed felt overwhelmed by all he had seen, and thought a return to the comparative tranquillity of the sand plain would rejuvenate his stunned senses. The sensation he got going back through the portal which linked the main complex to the space ship chamber only added to the build up of tension he was feeling, and he hurried on through the machinery hall to the end wall, looking for the lift which would whisk him up to a saner world.

As he approached the point where he had entered the hall, the wall slid back revealing the lift cavity and he hurried in, almost fearful the lift might go without him.

The row of eleven patches still gently glowed, and without hesitation he placed a palm on the topmost patch, and waited for the lift to complete its action.

Looking back a few moments later, he felt sure it was one of the side walls of the lift which had opened, but then he may have turned around when he touched the lift activating patch. Jed entered the passageway and strode out confidently, looking forward to open skies and the tranquillity of the sand plain.

He had been walking for some minutes when he got a sinking feeling. By now he should have reached the outer barrier, but the passage continued on, and then curved over to the left. There had been no curve in the passage on the way in. He stopped. He could go back, but that would only lead to the lift.

There was nothing for it, he would have to walk on, and hope there was another way out of the complex, although he had a nasty feeling he was going to be disappointed.

The passage narrowed down until he could only just squeeze through, and then opened out into a brightly lit room. As soon as he had entered the passage opening closed behind him, and he felt really trapped for the first time. The light in the room slowly faded until he could hardly see the walls, and then a blue violet luminescence flooded in, deepening into extreme ultra violet. He could feel it at the back of his eyes rather than actually see it, and it hurt.

Slowly he lost all sensation in his limbs, although his body remained upright, and then his vision went and he seemed to be floating in a nothingness, somewhere else.

Slowly his vision came back, the walls wavered a bit as though they were made of some strange liquid, and then steadied. He was aware of being aware, but he could not feel any sensation from his body, which was still standing upright like a frozen tableau.

A tingling began in his toes and fingers, quickly spreading to his trunk, and then he was whole again, and could move. As he turned his head to the right he found the wall had disappeared, exposing a passage. There was no where else to go.

The curve in the passageway began quite gently, tightening into a rising spiral as he walked on, and getting narrower the higher he went. He had never really suffered from claustrophobia before, but he was beginning to get the idea.

The expected blank wall confronted him as the passage ended, only this time the end wall was decorated with a symbol, a raised glowing gold star.

In the cramped space he turned his head to look back the way he had come, only to find that the passage had now shrunk so much that he would be unable to squeeze along it if he tried. Jed realized it was only an illusion, or was it?

He did not feel inclined to try and go back in case it was real, and the confined feeling was getting worse by the minute. An unsteady hand reached out and touched the star.

The end wall did not slide back as he had expected it to do, instead it just dissolved like a mist hit by the early morning sun, and he was through to the room beyond.

The centre of the room was taken up by a long curved desk or control console, its sloping surface covered in symbols laid out in neat rows, and at the back of this was a raised section with more symbols, each with its own softly glowing patch of light beneath it.

Above the desk, three, four metre square viewing screens were suspended, at least, that was what Jed thought they were, as their surfaces were lit with a faint iridescent glow, as if waiting to be made active.

In front of the desk was a chair, the like of which he had never seen before. It reminded him of a very elaborate space vehicle seat which would encase and protect the sitter against violent manoeuvres.

The over elaborate seat raised a chuckle as he surveyed the various complicated bits and pieces which adorned it, wondering what possible use they could have.

Around the walls stood various other machines, box-like consoles, and a series of plinths with the strange transparent stasis fields above them, hovering in and out of existence like a badly set up hologram.

The room itself had a pleasant warm welcoming feel about it, giving him the impression that it was pleased to be occupied, and that was when he began to wonder if he had somehow been controlled or steered into his present situation.

There did not seem to be any other exits from the room, and when he looked back to where he had come in, that too had disappeared. The usual fear flash of entrapment, which he expected, failed to happen, and he became more convinced than ever that something or someone was exerting some degree of control over him.

There was little he could do about the situation, so he just accepted it as no harm had come to him so far, and if harm had been intended, there had been plenty of opportunities for it to have happened.

Jed took off his net bag and placed it next to the seat, noticing that the food plums were still in good condition despite the rough time they must have had.

Perhaps the delicate skins of the plums were not so delicate after all, and it was an enzyme in his mouth which made them burst open so easily. He suddenly felt like one, and purposefully ran the end of his finger firmly across the skin several times before placing it in his mouth.

When he looked, it had left no mark, but the moment the plum was safely encased within his mouth, its heady aromatic juices spilled out, hitting his taste buds with delicious sensory stimulation.

Realizing his food stocks were slowly going down and there was nowhere to put the food pod down where it could produce more plums, his main concern should have been how to get back to the sand plain. The urge to do so was strangely missing, and that worried him too.

For the time being, there was not much he could do about the situation, so he eased himself into the over elaborate seating arrangement before the main control console, to relax for a moment and think things over.

He would have leapt to his feet, except he was not quick enough as the seat became alive around him, slowly reforming itself to fit his body contours perfectly. Jed's face lit up with what would have passed for a smile in his old body, as he realized that the seat was designed to cater for different body shapes, and had to change to accommodate his.

So who else had used it? And where were they now?

While he was trying to find a rational explanation for his cognition, the central screen lit up showing a brilliant star field in full three dimensions, and he had to resist the feeling of falling out of his seat and into the apparent realism of deep space. He watched in fascination, as the star field rushed towards him, the peripheral stars disappearing off the edge of the screen as he plunged ever deeper into space.

The scene continued to expand until a bright sun began to fill the centre of the screen, and then the picture froze.

At the same time as a pair of cross hairs appeared, centred just left of the sun, a light patch, or 'pad' as Jed thought of it, on the top left of the desk began to blink on and off.

He tentatively placed one finger on the pad, and as his finger moved, the cross hairs on the screen followed.

Instinctively, he moved the cross hairs to the centre of the sun, and then the screen to his left lit up with a plan view of the sun's planetary system. The cross hairs on the sun now disappeared and reappeared on the left-hand screen, and another pad began to blink, next to the first one.

It did not take Jed long to realize that he could roam the heavens, choose a sun, view it's system, select a planet in that system, and then, after a bit of experimentation to find the right pads, get a magnified view of that planet's surface.

What almost frightened him was the extremely close detail of the surface he could obtain, and in what appeared to be real time. Or was it a recording? He thought not.

He could see insects crawling about on what seemed to be a tangled slimy moss-like growth, draped over a half submerged rock which was sticking out of a pool of some indescribable bubbling liquid. He wondered if he really tried, he would be able to call up the stench the scene suggested, but thought better of it.

It was obvious to Jed that he had just been coached in how to use the control desk, but by whom, and why? Was he supposed to wander around the universe, seeking out new life forms and then somehow bring them back to the menagerie in the specimen halls? As interesting as the exercise had been, he did not like the idea of being a celestial fisherman, locating specimens for someone's collection.

After several fascinating hours exploring the universe, Jed felt hungry and left the comfort of his seat to retrieve a food plum, finding that he only had five left.

He still could not understand his lack of concern about the dwindling food stocks, normally he would have been frantic at this stage, and desperately searching for alternatives, not that the room he was in had anything to offer. Or did it?

Jed slowly walked around the control room, inspecting the numerous devices which lined its walls, most of which gave no indication as to their function, much to his frustration.

'If the control desk was anything to go by,' he mused, 'I should be able to work out what some of these machines do.' As he approached a gap between the machines, a section of wall slid back revealing another room beyond.

A long bench like structure lay along one wall. A small table with a viewing screen, complete with chair, but not so elaborate as the one he had just vacated, sat in one corner, while a device not unlike something he had seen in the machinery room, filled the other. A one metre square section of floor was slightly raised and had a soft glow shimmering on its surface, but, tempted as he was, he resisted the idea of stepping onto it until he had figured out what it did.

A much smaller platform on the bench, with a hood above it, attracted his attention, reminding him of the stasis field encapsulating machines he had seen earlier in the lower halls, except that the hazy 'field' was missing.

On the right-hand side of the platform a small raised section glowed, similar to the larger square on the floor.

Did the glow represent an invitation to do something?

'That's how the touch pads on the control desk seemed to work during the demonstration,' he thought, 'so perhaps this is the same sort of thing.'

Jed stood looking at the glowing plate, trying to think of something he could put on it for a test which he did not need for his survival. One of the precious fruits came to mind, but was rejected, and then he remembered the net bag.

The entrance to his 'rest room' as he saw it, was obvious, as it was the only piece of free wall which had nothing against it, and was big enough for a doorway.

The other gaps, between the resting bench, the desk, and the machine he wanted to try, were filled with short lengths of shelving, made of the same material as the rest of the room. It gave the impression that the whole thing had been moulded in one operation, the other items added as an after thought by someone who had failed to read the instructions.

Approaching the hidden doorway, a section of wall obediently slid back and he was in the control room again. The net bag had one or two straggly ends sticking out, and after a bit of a struggle, he managed to chew one of them off.

Returning to what he thought might be the stasis machine, Jed placed the little piece of cord like tendril Tree had made for him on the glowing plate, and waited for something to happen. Keeping his attention on the now soggy piece of cord, he failed to notice for a moment a small patch on the desk, softly blinking on and off.

Jed touched the patch hesitantly, and then jumped back as the hood began to lower and the little piece of cord disappeared from sight beneath it.

After a few seconds, the hood returned to its former position, and then proceeded to slide sideways to the other end of the desk. Again it lowered itself, and when it returned to its parked position, the piece of cord was entrapped for ever in a transparent energy cage. Next to the newly arrived stasis block, another touch pad was blinking its invitation.

Jed's initial impulse was to touch the pad, but he withheld his over eager finger while he tried to reason out what might happen if he did.

Why would his rest room have a personal 'encapsulation machine' when there were plenty down in the complex? Perhaps he was unable to get down to the lower depths of the complex any more.

Jed hurried back to the control room, located what he thought was the section of wall through which he had come earlier from the passageway, and began searching for anything which would open it. There was nothing. The section of wall which had allowed him access now remained as solid as the rest of the control room walls.

Jed could feel frustration building up again as he realized his options were diminished still further.

As far as he could tell, he had access to the control room and what he thought of as his rest room, and that was it. No more roaming about on the planet's unpredictable but interesting surface, no more glorious sunsets, not even a wander around the vast halls of specimens.

He returned to the rest room, and as he approached the bench, the pad next to the stasis block began to blink again, reminding him that some action was waiting to be taken.

Impatience rather than logic drove his finger down onto the pad with a little more force than was strictly necessary, and the hood began to lower over the transparent block. It paused there for a few seconds, rose again, and travelled across to the other end of the bench.

Again it began its slow descent to the surface of the bench, and upon ascending to its parked position, revealed a soggy piece of cord, identical to that which resided in the stasis block at the other end of the bench.

Somewhere, deep in the recesses of Jed's mind, pieces of data he had been subconsciously collecting over the past few days suddenly realigned themselves, and a realization of staggering proportions formed. It was an ephemeral thing, lasting but a few microseconds before it receded out of his mental reach, but he knew he had had a cognition on something of momentous importance.

He stood looking at the sad piece of cord for some minutes, and then reached forward to pick it up. It seemed real, and felt just like its original before it was locked up in the stasis block. But why would he need to duplicate a piece of ....?

The penny dropped with a resounding clang. Jed almost ran out to the net bag and removed one of his precious plums. Did he dare risk losing one? If he did, it would only bring his inevitable starvation one meal forward, but there again, it might just be his salvation.

He placed the plum on the glowing raised section of the bench, touched the illuminated pad, and silently said a little prayer, not that he really believed it would help.

The hood lowered over the plum, retracted, and moved over to the other end of the bench. Meanwhile, the stasis block encasing the piece of cord slid back into an opening in the wall, and disappeared from view.

When the hood had descended and then returned to its original position, a new stasis block now shimmered on the bench, with the plum locked inside it.

Hardly able to believe his good fortune, Jed tentatively touched the glowing pad next to the block, and when the machine had completed its cycle a glistening new food plum lay waiting on the bench. The skin ruptured as the enzymes in his mouth went to work, and he nearly spilled some of the delectable juice as a grin swept across his face.

With the food problem solved, Jed felt a lot better, but he still did not like the idea that he was no longer free to roam at will about the complex, or the world outside.

The raised section of floor in the corner of the room still glowed gently, inviting him to do something with it. Being large enough to stand on was no guarantee that it was intended for such a purpose, but he could not think what other use it might have. Would it make a duplicate of him? He thought not, as there was no hood above it.

With a degree of trepidation, Jed stepped onto the platform, and the glow went out as it slowly began to rise. He was ready to jump off if it looked as though he would be crushed against the ceiling, but a hole had opened above him, so he centred himself on the platform to avoid being hit by the now fast approaching edge of a shaft.

Once the platform had entered the shaft, it accelerated upwards at a considerable speed, as he could tell from the rate at which the walls sped by, and then he was out in the cool open air, the sky splashed with sunset colours.

As it stopped, Jed stepped off the lift into a circular enclosure, and noticed the glow had returned to the platform's surface, indicating he thought, that it was now ready to take him down again.

He was at the top of a tall tower, positioned at one corner of the vast complex below, the flat top of which stretched off for as far as he could see, dark and sinister against the paler sand colour of the surrounding desert area.

An encircling wall at waist height alleviated a little of the vertigo Jed felt as he looked down from the dizzying height of the tower. He still could not rationalize why he felt so uncomfortable in such a situation, when he was used to the free fall of a space walk around his old ship.

He wished there had been a breeze, everything was too still and quiet, and it gave an eerie feeling to the scene as if the whole world had been locked still in time.

Leaning on the parapet, looking out over the sand plains, Jed got to thinking about what had happened to him over the last ... ? How long had it been? He found it difficult to quantify the time since leaving the fast disintegrating ore ship which had been his home for so long.

He somehow felt that a guiding hand, or perhaps something a little stronger, had been involved in what had taken place.

The ship should have picked up the meteorite storm, it had never failed before. The escape pod just had to hit those few lone rocks on landing, wrecking the very remote chance of the homing beacon signal getting through, when there had been plenty of clear space and soft sand all around.

Even the direction he had taken was not wholly of his own volition, a little nudge here, a suggestion there. His body just happened to expire on the exact spot required to initiate Tree, and Tree then provided him with a body more suitable to the inhospitable environment the planet was blessed with.

Something wanted him to find the edifice, and helped him along the way when he faltered. He had been given the 'grand tour' of the complex, guided up to the control room, shown how things worked, but not actually asked to do anything specific.

'So just what the hell is going on?' He tried to mouth the words, just to hear the sounds, but he had no larynx to speak of, so it sounded more like a series of grunts.

Jed must have been lost in his thoughts far longer than he realized, for the sun had almost set when he came out of his reverie, and the lift platform now shone with a warm welcoming glow in the twilight, inviting him down to his room.

Back in his room, Jed thought it snug and comfortable, despite its sparse furnishings, probably engendered by the warm welcoming feeling which pervaded the space.

Although he had recently eaten, the temptation to try the 'plum reproducer' was too much, and he causally brushed a finger across the touch pad, and waited for his meal to appear.   It tasted just as good as the last one, and he wondered what would happen if he doubled or tripled his intake. Would he put weight on? Or was his new body designed to cope with excessive gastronomic indulgence? He felt so full now the idea of another plum was almost abhorrent, so he had his answer.

The bench like bed looked a little more comfortable than the sand he had slept on for the last few nights, but only by a small margin. Jed sat on its edge, swung his legs up, and lay down. He should have been expecting it, but it caught him by surprise when it began to move beneath him.

At first, gentle ripples ran up and down its length, to be joined by a strange sensation as cross ripples became more predominant, easing away the tension.

Somehow the bed sensed his most important motor muscles, and worked on them until they softened and he began to feel sleepy, then the bed reshaped itself to cocoon him softly in its gentle folds, the light in the room dimmed to the faintest of glows and he slipped into the deepest sleep he had known for many a long night.

Dreams came and went, most of which were insignificant and bore little relationship to his recent experiences, but one did stick in his mind, and he remembered most of it when he awoke, feeling refreshed and eager to see what the day would bring, not that he was sure what part of day it was in the isolation of the complex.

Hardly aware of eating his first plum of the day, Jed recalled the dream. He had been sitting at the main control desk and somehow he knew what all the myriad of symbols meant. His fingers flew over the desk top, calling up pictures of the various creatures stored below in the depths of the complex, searching for one particular type.

At last he had located the species, but the variations on the theme were so numerous that he could not decide which one was best suited for the purpose. But then he could not remember clearly what the purpose was.

A viewing screen lit up showing an area of what looked like forest, but the trees were a hideous caricature of those he had known in real life, and looked repulsive.

Tall, and flimsy to the point where they could hardly support their own weight, they kept crashing down before they reached maturity. The forest floor was metres deep in tangled broken tree trunks, affording little support for new trees as the loosely knitted fibrous debris of the fallen trunks crumbled and shifted at the slightest pressure.

He knew that something was needed to clear the ever growing depth of litter, so that new growths could secure a sure footing in the ground, and become self supporting.

In his dream, Jed kept scanning the sample banks, looking for a creature which would consume the dead wood, but not attack the living trees. A metre long grey worm-like creature, with a set of mandibles which looked capable of crushing rock, looked promising, and he selected it.

He touched the keypads to begin the duplication process, selected a suitable carrier to hold his new creations and..... the dream faded out.

Something clicked in the back of Jed's mind, he almost knew what it was, and then it was gone.

Six:
Who's there?

WITH NOTHING ELSE to do, Jed went through to the main control room and began to examine the strange looking equipment lining the walls. None of it suggested what it might be intended for, with the exception of one unit.

An alpha numeric key pad sat on a small shelf which jutted out from the wall, above which a lifeless viewing screen stared blankly back at him. Jed could not remember seeing it when he had looked around the previous day, and wondered if it had been added during his sleep period.

The numbers and letters were just the same as those on the ship, and such were peculiar to his race of people. A cold shiver rippled down his spine.

'Either the last person here was of my people, or there is some intelligence here.' Tree had been able to see his mental image pictures, and act on them, and so had something else, if the keyboard was anything to go by. It might just be a very clever computer with an advanced sensing device, or was it something else? He did not like the idea of that.

So far, he had considered the whole complex was purely mechanical, albeit a bright one, but the thought that there was an 'intelligence' present unnerved him a little.

Not thinking that anything would happen because the screen was unlit, he idly tapped in 'Hello.' and stood back.

'Hello Jed.' instantly flashed up in bright green letters on the screen above the keyboard.

'Bloody hell.' Jed was badly shaken by the response.

His fingers nervously tapped out 'Who are you?'

The screen remained resolutely blank, despite several permutations of the same basic query, so he gave up for the time being, intending to try again when he had formulated a few more suitably crafty questions.

Looking at the main control desk, Jed realized that he had gained one positive benefit from his dreams, he could still remember what the symbols meant, except for a very few on the raised ledge above the main desk area.

Recalling the crumbling trees of his dream, he mounted the super seat and brought the main screen to life, the brilliant reality of the star field giving him a brief feeling of vertigo as the illusion of flying through space enveloped him.

He wanted to find the forested planet in his dream, but then realized the dream had begun in the forest, so he had no idea what the sun of the system looked like.

A twinkling blue star caught his attention, and using the cross hairs, he centred in on the planetary system. Four worlds out from the sun, a white ball of cloud looked unusual enough to bear investigation, and he homed in on it, increasing the magnification until the water vapour covered planet filled the screen. Thick dirty clouds rushed at him as the viewing device drove down towards the surface, and then the motion stopped.

Turbulent grey clouds encompassed the world, holding it in perpetual twilight, making finite details difficult to observe.

A thick oily sea sent a series of pathetically weak ripples onto a shore line of greasy looking rounded pebbles.

A few patches of grey green slime mould had tried to colonize some of the pebbles, but either the stones were too smooth, or the mould lacked the necessary means of getting a firm grip on the slippery surface.

A small wavelet nudged one patch of mould, and it peeled off its host pebble, floating away on the receding water.

Seconds later, the surface of the turbid sea was broken as something thrust a black shiny snout at the floating patch of mould, and it was gone.

Jed swung the view around to look at the land. The pebble bank gave way to a mass of dark jagged rocks which had crashed down from the towering cliffs above. Even as he watched, the ground gave a series of shudders, and another section of cliff detached itself, falling some fifty metres to shatter into fragments as it met its predecessors below.

He could see no sign of plant life on the barren landscape, and wondered if plants had yet to migrate from ocean to land, or if they had existed, but died out due to unfavourable atmospheric conditions and the lack of adequate light.

Using the touch pads, Jed swung the 'viewer' up over the gaunt riven cliffs to see what the terrain above was like.

Huge basaltic lava flows had spread across the land, covering it in frozen waves and ripples of glistening hard rock and hiding whatever lay beneath. The viewer sped inland, pausing at an area of deep sand dunes, one edge of which was fringed with rounded pebbles.

From his knowledge of geology, Jed knew for this much sand to have formed, and by the presence of smooth pebbles at its edge, there must have been a lot of quite violent water action at some time in the past to have worn the rocks down.

The viewer moved on, and a crater some four kilometres across came into view. The sharpness of its sides and the type of debris around its perimeter indicated a massive impact, most likely from a large meteorite. Several other craters of differing sizes swept by, as the viewer headed towards a long range of mountains on the horizon.

Jed thought this must be a relatively young world, halted in its development by some enormous catastrophe, and having now decayed to a reasonably stable state. It would seem future advancement of living species were now restricted by the altered environment.

In the far distance, a long line of smoke and fine ash slowly drifted like a dirty ribbon across the hazy horizon, adding to the already polluted and over laden atmosphere. The volcanic action responsible for the atmosphere's increasing burden of detritus came into view some moments later.

Internal pressure from shifting tectonic plates had blown a section of mountainside into oblivion; the resulting rift was now pouring forth a constant stream of thick red treacle-like lava onto the plain below, noxious gasses bursting from the bubbling sticky mass as it rolled along.

Leaving the fuming volcanic rent in the mountain, the viewer flew on to a larger range of mountains Jed could see in the distance. These had a lower plateau of limestone cliffs fringing their base, and this confirmed his view that the planet had once been in a viable life supporting state.

He took the viewer up the mountain, past the shiny black up thrust of age old bed rock, to its peak, now covered in a blanket of dirty grey snow and ice. From this vantage point, he had a good view of the desolate terrain below, and of a planet which had nearly died.

From what he had observed, and from his not inconsiderable knowledge, he worked out what must have happened to the unfortunate world.

At one time, life must have been prolific in the seas; hence the massive chalk cliffs at the mountain's base. The presence of rounded water worn stones meant that at one time there had been rumbustious seas pounding the coastline, grinding the rocks into fine particles to form the huge sand dunes he had seen earlier. Heavy seas, and a rising and falling tide, needed a satellite in orbit around the planet to generate them, and he had not noticed one when he swept the viewer in from the sun.

Jed reasoned that at one time the planet had been progressing along its evolutionary road, warmed by its nearby sun, its satellite moon pulling on the oceans to form the necessary tides to wear and sculpt its shores, so releasing minerals for the growth of marine life.

The probability was that a rouge meteorite had hit the moon, shattering it into several pieces, the orbits of which had decayed and then rained down on the surface below. The resultant mass of fine dust this generated would have been enough to mask the sunlight from the planet for ages.

The impact would have given the necessary release to any underground stresses which had built up, opening deep fissures and loosening volcanic vents, from which would pour huge amounts of carbon and sulphur dioxide, and yet more dust. The overall effect of this would be to create a 'greenhouse' situation, where heat from the sun would be trapped, the temperature would escalate, and the atmosphere would then hold more water, adding to the problem.

Most of the dust would have been washed out of the atmosphere in time, leaving only the finest of aerosols and water vapour to shield the planet from life giving sunlight.

The whole world had ground to an evolutionary and geophysical halt, with nothing to kick it back into a cyclic system, which was necessary for life to evolve and progress.

The viewing system was so real that Jed had to consciously pull himself out of it, and back into the real time and space of the control room. Realizing that he had been straining forward all the time, he lay back in his seat, which then readjusted itself to accommodate his new position.

Jed somehow felt sorry for the unfortunate planet and the remnants of life which still struggled to exist there, and instinctively wanted to take some action to alter its state.

'What we need to do,' he thought, 'is to give the oceans a massive injection of algae. That would absorb the carbon dioxide, lock up the carbon, and release oxygen. Once the carbon dioxide level comes down, the temperature will drop, and it'll rain. When the cloud cover is lessened, the sunlight will get through and things can begin to grow again.'

He ran the sequence through again, it seemed reasonable, although he realized the time scale would be enormous.

Suddenly, something clicked in his mind as a final piece of data slotted into place, and he nearly leapt out of the seat.

Jed felt dizzy and unreal as the full realization of what the complex was all about and his reason for being there became crystal clear.

'it's not a bloody collector's museum; it's a generating station for populating the universe!' He sank back in the seat, soaked in a cold sweat. The seat, noticing the increase in moisture, opened pores in its outer covering and gently absorbed the excess fluid away from its charge, tainting the surrounding air with a subtle trace of aromatheriac essence to induce a state of calm.

Jed could hardly believe his discovery, yet it all seemed reasonable when he thought about it. All the bits and pieces added up to make one coherent whole, and it made sense.

Then he realized the responsibility of such a post, and went cold again.

The desk with its myriad of symbolized touch pads, the three huge screens, and the as yet little understood machines around the control room walls, all took on a new significance of frightening proportions, and he wondered if he was competent enough to do the job. What if he made a mistake?

Just getting one little thing wrong could have a knock on effect which could wipe out all life on a whole world.

Jed tried to relax in his seat, but he could still feel a certain amount of tension in his body. As he wriggled about trying to relieve it, the seat began to subtly massage his muscles where they contacted the pseudonamic covering, easing the stress away.

As the last tiny tremors left his body, Jed was able to think clearly again. He still found it hard to come to terms with the situation, yet he could not refute the basic concept.

Then he remembered the keyboard.

'Hello.' He tapped in carefully.

'Hello Jed.'

'Have I been guided here?'

'Yes.'

'By whom?' There was no answer; the screen remained blank after the previous answer had slowly faded away.

'Do I have a purpose here?'

'Yes.'

'What is that purpose?'

'You know what your purpose here is.'

'Are you here to help me?'

'Yes.'

'Then why don't you answer my questions?'

'Your questions will be answered where it will be helpful.'

Jed noticed the subtle avoidance of 'I', or any reference to 'self', which would have told him a lot.

'Do you think I am capable of what is required of me?'

'You have been chosen.'

'Can you make mistakes?'

'No.'

'Can I make mistakes?'

'The risk factor is very low and will diminish still further with time and practice.' Jed was getting nowhere.

'If I have a problem, will you help me solve it?'

'Certain technical questions which are deemed within your capabilities will be answered.'

'I understand my main purpose is to correct faults on worlds which have survival problems, does this also include seeding new worlds which are without life forms?'

'Correct.'

'What if I get it wrong?'

'You correct it.'

'When do I begin this work?'

'When you are ready.'

'What is your name, how do I address you?'

'There is no need to.'

'You're a reticent little sod, aren't you?'

'Is that a question or comment?'

'Consider it a question.' Jed replied, feeling he might be getting somewhere.

'The question is not understood, please rephrase it.'

'Bollocks.' Jed was now getting really wound up, his patience stretched to the limit. In a way, he felt happy he still had some good old human traits.

As the screen went blank he got up to stretch his legs, and thinking back on the matter, he felt a little ashamed for his outburst, it was hardly called for.

Jed returned to his seat and looked up at the main screen. The swirling dirty clouds were still there and the land still remained in semi darkness. He needed to know how to get back to this world in the future after he had located the correct algae for its oceans, but how was he to do that?

The obvious answer was to ask 'it'. (as yet, he had not chosen a reference name for 'it', although he had thought of many).

He felt a bit reluctant to use the keyboard so soon after his outburst, but if he wanted an answer there was little option.

'Hello.'

'Hello Jed.'

'Sorry about my rudeness just now.'

'What rudeness was that Jed?'

'Oh forget it, I have a question for you.'

Jed waited for a moment, fully expecting something to come up on the screen. But nothing did.

'I have located a planet which needs some attention, how can I get back to it once it's off screen?'

'Run the cross hairs back to the planet's sun. Touch the pad which is now lit, and the co-ordinates will be recorded. You may also key in your own reference if you wish. To return to the system, touch the pad, select the co-ordinates you require or your own reference, and press the pad again.'

Jed looked back at the main desk. A touch pad on the far end of the raised section was glowing softly.

'Thank you.' Jed felt like being courteous.

'You are welcome.' The screen went blank.

With the cross hairs correctly aligned on the sun, Jed touched the pad. A small screen built into the surface of the far end of the desk, lit up, and beneath it an equally small key board appeared. He could not recall having seen either item before, and wondered why.

A row of symbols ran across the top of the screen, and he added 'cloud world' after them using the keyboard, which he found a bit awkward as his fingers were so big compared to the smaller keys of the mini board.

Jed wondered if the details of the planet he were stored somewhere within the complex and called up when needed, or was he seeing it in real time, and if so, how?

After his tussle with 'it', Jed felt the first pangs of hunger, and decided he would eat the food plums he had brought with him rather than waste them. They were still as fresh as the day the food pod had made them, and he wondered just how long they would last. Perhaps he would keep one back just to see.

The search for a suitable algae began. He had found the controls which allowed him to view the specimen halls, but it took a little time before he became proficient at using them. Locating the plant hall, he scanned along the lines of growths until he came to the slime moulds and lichen section, but the sheer number of variations was overwhelming.

Eventually, he found three types which he thought might survive in the thick soup-like waters and half light of the planet.

The stasis blocks in which they were held had a series of symbols on each base pedestal, and he noted these down on the small keyboard and screen, which had so mysteriously appeared on the end of his desk earlier. He later referred to this device as his universal note pad, as it had so many functions, and more being revealed with use.

Jed had no scientific reason for choosing the three types of algae, and he had no idea what the waters of the planet contained, but somehow he felt they were right. The choice was done purely on a hunch, as if his attention had been drawn to them somehow.

Whether this was an innate skill he had not been aware of before, or something the complex had added to his repertoire, he had no idea, but it seemed to work.

He decided to select all three types of algae, feeling sure that at least one of them would survive, but he knew he would not live long enough to see the result.

It was while Jed was asking 'it' how to operate the duplicating process that he happened to mention the fact that he would not be able to see the results of his work.

'You can use the simulator; it is ninety percent plus accurate.'

Instructions followed, and Jed returned to the main desk, and impatiently fed the data into his note pad.

The screen on the right lit up, and he was looking at the dark grey green oily swell of a sluggish ocean. The algae data was added and the time sequence set to fifty, he assumed it was years of whatever planetary system he was working on. Each touch of the pad advanced the process, and it was many presses later before he saw the clouds lighten and the waters take on a faint tinge of blue.

Patches of blue sky appeared eventually, and the shoreline took on a new look as various forms of growing things began to advance up the beach in little trickles, looking more like plants as they invaded the rocky area below the cliffs.

Creeping things hungrily devoured the gelatinous blobs of a jelly like creature which was occasionally washed up on the shoreline, while something a little larger with a wicked set of mandibles, ate them in turn.

Looking out to sea, Jed could see something very large cruising along some fifty metres out, its bow wave leaving a white foaming wake as multiple fins drove the sea creature in search of food.

Jed reset the time pad for one thousand years, and knew he had been right with his choice of algae as life burgeoned forth with every touch of the pad.

A view from the mountains showed a green and pleasant land, well populated with plants and a weird and wonderful selection of creatures to feed on them, and each other.

Considering the pictures were only generated within a piece of machinery, and then only from data supplied, Jed was very impressed with the quality, not being able to tell mock-up from reality.

He was satisfied that he had made the right choice, and gave instructions for the algae to be duplicated, watching with interest as the hoods descended over the chosen stasis blocks in the plant hall. He would have liked to follow the sequence right through, but it was too quick for him, and lost track of the hoods as they retracted and sped off through a hole in the end wall of the repository, the viewer refusing to follow them.

Jed wanted more data about the whole project, but thought it best to pose the questions on an increasing gradient of inquisitiveness rather than come out bluntly with the main ones. After the usual courteous opening preamble, he began.

'How long will it take to grow on the algae?'

'Not long. It is duplicated, not grown.'

'How does the system know how much to make?'

'It is calculated from the data you fed in.'

'How long will it take to get there, and by what means, and will it still be viable after a long journey?'

'By this time tomorrow. It will be loaded into cylinders and dispatched. There will be no degeneration of viability in the short journey time.'

'How will it be dispatched?'

'That has been answered.'

'How will the cylinders be transported to the planet?'

'It is beyond your scientific knowledge. You would not understand.'

'Bloody try me?'

'Your question is not understood. Is it a question?'

Jed swallowed hard. He was getting nowhere, as before, but he did notice one thing, the answers to his triple question were stilted, and came back rather mechanically he thought. A sentient being would have phrased it rather differently.

'By what means will the transporter be propelled?'

'It is not propelled in the sense you mean.'

'In any bloody sense, how does the transporter get from here to the receiving planet?'

'By creating a time warp in space.'

'How is a time warp in space created?'

'By spatial distortion at the start point and the end point. Time between these two points does not exist as they are not anchor points of solidity, so they are one and the same.'

'Thank you, I understood that.'

'That is not possible. Your knowledge base is insufficient.'

'Would you please explain the theory a little more?'

'The data will be of no use to you. This question and any variation on the basic theme will no longer be accepted.'

'Stuff you, arrogant little sod.' Jed had tapped the words in before he could monitor what he said, but he did feel better for doing so.

The screen had gone blank, and he thought he had experienced enough mental tussles for one day. Leaving the control room, Jed went to the lift platform in his rest room for a breath of fresh air, not that the air in the room was stale, but he though it a bit too pure, he needed to be in touch with something real, a world he understood, for a while.

As he walked over to the parapet, the last tiny section of the sinking sun dipped below the horizon, the sky lit up in a series of brilliant coloured flashes, and then night rushed in. He thought he felt a gentle breeze brush across his face, but then, perhaps not. He was hoping for too much.

The stars sprang into being as if a celestial hand had flipped a switch somewhere, dazzlingly bright and sharp.

A very faint metallic dusty smell tainted the air, and Jed was instantly reminded of his tramp across the barren sand plains before he encountered the enigmatic Tree.

Looking back, he found it hard to understand how he had kept going when his body was breaking down, its organs pushed well beyond their design limits, and failing one by one. He must have had a little help from somewhere.

A bright pinpoint of light moved among the stars, a faint thin vapour trail fading out behind it. Someone was up there, using an ion drive, and Jed wondered what had happened to his old ship. It had been well off course when he left it, and would probably never be seen again, except perhaps by a very distant alien race. What would they make of the huge hulk, stuffed full of mineral ore, and no pilot?

How the complex had extracted the necessary information from his mind, and then constructed the keyboard communication system was still beyond his comprehension. The most baffling part was the use of language.

Even the best computers he knew of had a hard time of it trying to decipher technical questions, and get the answers right. Somehow the complex had cooked up the gadget in the control room, complete with 'it', and yet, had taken everything he could throw at it, in its stride.

He had noticed the little nuances of certain words and phrases went over its electronic head, and that gave him some comfort in a seemingly perfect and fault free world.

'Funny,' he mused, 'man has always struggled for perfection, and now I'm in it, I'm not so sure I like it.'

A distant sun went nova, and for a short while Jed gazed in wonderment at the sight. It made him feel insignificant.

The night air had acquired a slight chill, and Jed returned to the pristine but comfortable room the complex had so kindly provided him with. He was not ready for sleep yet, despite the long and exciting day. After eating one of the few remaining original food plums, he sat on the edge of the bench bed wondering what to do next.

On a section of wall opposite him a viewing screen came to life. It seemed to be part of the wall itself, which was why he had not noticed it before. A soft melodious tone sounded.

'*A selection of views from various planets has been assembled for your entertainment. Should you wish to see them, please touch the pad below the screen.*'

This was the first time he had heard a voice since he bemoaned his lot so long ago. It seemed strange to hear a voice after so long, and he wanted to hear it again.

Jed tried to speak, but only his whistling breath and a muffled grunt resulted for his troubles. Disappointed at his inability to speak, he leaned forward, touched the pad and sat back to enjoy what the complex had to offer.

Who, or whatever, had been responsible for putting the collection of moving views together must have had an artistic appreciation of some considerable degree, he thought.

Jed was quite moved by the sheer beauty of sunsets he would have been hard put to imagine, waterfalls many hundreds of metres high, the water almost reduced to mist by the time it had descended to ground level. Vast cloud-like shoals of multi coloured swimming creatures, all moving in perfect unison to some unspoken command, swirling in patterns so complicated that he was mesmerized by the movement, the interplay, the changing colours, the...

His eyelids were heavy, it was so pleasant to let them close.

As Jed's body slumped against the wall, the bench bed exuded two pseudo pods. One extended downwards to catch his legs and swing them up and around onto the bed, while the other one slipped up his back, cradling his head and lowering it gently to rest on a slightly raised section of the bed, so that his neck would not be strained while he slept.

Awaking from a deep and untroubled sleep, he was ready for the day. A food plum annulled his hunger, and he went into the control room fully intending to take on the recalcitrant 'it' once more.

The main viewing screen above the desk was glowing, so he took his seat in front of the control desk, and waited to see what would happen.

'A planet has been located which may need your attention, please view and assess.'

The unexpected voice made him jump, but then the screen came to life. It was if he were in some sort of vehicle, speeding through space towards a planet which grew bigger by the second, and then it plunged below the cloud layer and he could see the surface some ten metres below him.

The undulating ground, with a few rocks protruding timidly from its surface, seemed covered in grey green slime, but when he drew closer he could see it was a very fine and dense moss-like growth. Some patches seemed to be of a slightly different shade, and then he realized that it was not one continuous sheet, but many separate patches of different sizes, the edges of each one trying to gain more space by consuming its neighbour. The movement was very slow, but just discernible when he concentrated.

Using the touch pad, he sent the viewer up the first slope and paused at the top. Below, where the surface flattened out, a ten metre circle of something else held its ground.

It looked much like a huge circle of very old yellow wrinkled leather, with a small crimson bulbous hump in the middle. At its extremity, there was a clear five centimetre wide circle of dark brown crumbly ground, as if nothing wanted to colonize it.

The moss came up to the edge of the circle, and there it stopped. Jed thought perhaps the edge of the leather circle thing exuded something to discourage any intrusion of its space, but as he was not actually there, he was unable to prove the point.

He swung the viewer upwards as he heard the hoop and whistle of leathery wings. A hideous creation lumbered along some ten metres above the ground, giving the impression that it was only just able to fly, even on a good day, and landed hesitatingly in the top wispy branches of a gnarled and twisted tree-like growth.

The body of the flying creature looked like a skeleton, tightly covered with a thin layer of translucent dirty skin, which where it covered the long and sinuous neck, did so in a series of ring-like folds, suggesting the neck could be extended to at least twice its normal length.

It had difficulty in keeping its balance, wobbling about uncertainly with the occasional rustle and flap of its wings, desperately trying to stay on its unsteady and flimsy perch.

The gnarled branches below the top of the tree began to slowly bend upwards in a vain attempt to encircle the flyer, but just in time the creature realized what was about to happen, and frantically launched itself into the air.

Before the frenziedly beating wings could generate enough forward speed to create lift, the monstrosity began to lose height, swooping down in the direction of the leather circle.

Jed thought he could hear the bones creak under the effort.

As the flying thing approached the centre of the leather circle, the bulbous hump in its middle opened in a parody of two voluptuous red lips, and a thin yellow tendril shot out to encircle the flyer. Jed could definitely hear the crunch of bones this time as the tendril tightened its grip, and then it was sucked back into the crimson hump.

The leather circle rippled a couple of times, the lips opened a fraction and spat out the beak of the flyer, which landed on the moss at the edge of the circle. The moss rose up, split open, and a long thin claw grabbed the beak and withdrew back into its hole in the ground, the moss flopping back as if nothing had happened.

Jed gulped, and moved the viewer upwards and forward, fast. As a range of hills came into view, he slowed the viewer down to look at a large outcrop of jumbled rocks.

Perched on a ledge, and matching the colour of the rocks exactly, a multi-limbed hump of something sat, with two eyes on the end of stalks drooped over the edge scanning the ground some two metres below. Two prehensile limbs held a piece of stone above the hump of the body, as if shielding it from something, but Jed could see nothing threatening in the rocks above.

Directly below the ledge, a pink worm-like thing protruded from the bare ground wriggling about energetically, and Jed was surprised that anything would risk advertising its presence so enthusiastically in such a hostile environment.

A scraping and rattling noise announced that something was approaching, and Jed moved the viewer back a little to take in a larger portion of the area.

Around the corner of the rock pile a crustaceous looking creature shuffled along, a dark brown wrinkled carapace matching the ground being all he could see of it.

No legs or other means of locomotion were visible, so he assumed that whatever propelled it along was safely tucked up under the all protecting carapace.

When the crustacean spotted the pink wriggling worm, it froze, and then very slowly edged forward to circle around it, with only the occasional click as one of it limbs hit a small stone. Having satisfied itself that the worm was probably a tasty meal, a single articulated appendage equipped with a pincer like claw, crept out from under the carapace.

Just as the claw was about to close on its target, the worm slid down into its hole and the creature above launched its missile, the rock dropping neatly onto the carapace below, shattering it into several pieces. The gelatinous goo within the carapace held the fragments together, so that when a long rope like appendage swept down from above, it was able to scope up the crushed remains in one piece.

Jed watched fascinated, as the hump on the ledge pulled in its prey and began to greedily suck out the contents from the shattered body, neatly placing the empty pieces of shell on the little pile of earlier conquests alongside it.

As the last piece of shell was sucked dry and discarded, the little pink worm came out of its hole again to continue its enticing dance of death.

Jed was unable to determine whether the pink worm and the hump on the ledge were two creatures working symbiotically, or if the worm was just an extension of the hump, which had somehow extended itself down through the rocks and into the ground beneath.

Symbiotic relationships were quite common in nature, as evidenced by the fungus and algae which together make up lichen, but he could not see what benefit the worm got out of the deal, so he favoured the latter.

Jed moved the viewer up the rocks and on to where a fumarole was sending its noxious yellow and brown gasses skywards. Sulphur had precipitated out from the vented gasses, and formed a thick bright yellow encrustation around the hot fuming hole. He sent the viewer in, not expecting to see anything alive in such a hostile environment, but life existed here too.

Tiny beetle-like insects scurried about, flaking the yellow sulphur off with minuscule mandibles and carrying it away to burrows cut into the miniature cliffs which surrounded the stinking fumer.

Crouched on the edge above the burrows, a hideous parody of a giant slug with a wrinkled and knobbly skin was fishing.

A single many jointed slender arm with two curved prongs on its end swept down among the beetles, attempting to scoop up a meal. The fixed prongs were at such a distance apart that only the largest beetles were caught, the smaller younger members of the colony slipping through the scoop to grow on, one day being large enough to be caught and consumed by the powerful crushing jaws of the fisher.

He moved the viewer on, searching for a different environment to complete his view of the planet.

A dark green sea heaved itself sluggishly against huge cliffs, trying to erode more space against glass hard basalt rocks which were as unyielding as the sea was tenacious.

Jed wondered if the viewer would go under water, this being a region worth looking at, as life usually began there.

The initial plunge below the waves shocked him as it was so realistic, and he found himself instinctively holding his breath. Down the viewer went, passing huge fronds of lurid green seaweed and long purple brown waving sheets of something he could not identify.

Seven:
Tooth and Claw

As the viewer plunged deeper still, the rough encrusted surface of a coral reef came into sight, with its hard abrasive appearance softened by groups of coloured fronds and tendrils. The reef seemed to be floating at a pre-set depth, until the viewer revealed a thin column attached to its underside, which disappeared down into the depths below.

It reminded Jed of a giant mushroom on a very thin extended stalk, but there the resemblance ended.

Scanning the reef to see if there were any mobile life forms present only revealed plant growths adorning the stony surface, and he was about to move on down to the sea bed, when a shoal of small swimming creatures swept into view and headed for what little shelter the reef afforded.

Several larger creatures with teeth laden snapping jaws corkscrewed their way through the water in pursuit of the shoal, which by now had split up and tried to hide as individuals among the waving fronds.

A few stragglers were picked off by the marauders who then left, spiralling their way down into the dark waters below, while the smaller swimmers regrouped and hesitatingly moved off as a shoal again. The shoal was so much smaller now, so Jed moved closer to see what had become of the rest of them, as the marauders had only taken a few.

The viewer stopped half a metre away from the reef surface, and then Jed saw what had happened to the rest of the little swimmers. Some were tightly wrapped in fronds, and a mere shadow of their former selves, while others were sticking halfway out of holes in the coral, and being slowly sucked in. He concluded that the coral must be a living organism, feeding on anything foolish enough to seek shelter in its beautiful but deadly mantle.

A shadow flickered across the reef and he backed the viewer away to see what had caused it, and get an overall picture of the coral creature.

The new intruder to the scene was a good two metres long with a sleek grey blue body, several sets of driving fins and a long snout. There were no visible eyes that he could see, but that did not seem to hinder the careful probing snout, which had extended out to form a small tube, from sucking the few still exposed little swimmers from the clutches of the reef creature.

The reef could do little to stop the robbery, in fact Jed thought it might have actually been a ploy to catch an even bigger meal. A couple of metres away from the larcenous interloper a section of the reef began to open, forming a slit like cave. The robber worked its way along the reef, sucking out the little swimmers from the holes which held them, saw something tempting within the cave, and pushed its snout in.

The water swirled around the cave opening as the robber was sucked in and the hinged section of the reef closed shut a lot faster than it had opened, only leaving a small portion of tail showing, and that too, soon disappeared from view.

Jed considered going down to the ocean floor, but thought he had seen enough to formulate a valid opinion on the state of the planet's life forms, and sent the viewer back up to the surface.

Not knowing how to switch it off, or even if it needed to be shut down, he lay back in his seat. As he took his hands off the desk, the screen went blank.

Whether it was his action which had ended the viewing or the complex sensed it was no longer necessary to keep the video link open, mattered little to Jed. He not only felt tired, but exhausted from viewing the planet and its life forms, and wanted to rest for a while, and get back to reality.

His leaden eyelids had closed and he was just drifting off into a pleasant relaxing sleep when the 'ping' of the enunciator snapped him wide awake, and he felt annoyed.

'Earlier you expressed a wish to see the algae you selected arrive at its destination. It is now due. If you wish to see the dispersal, please activate the centre screen.'

Jed leaned forward lethargically and touched the pad. The screen displayed the cloud covered planet of yesterday, and as he watched, a section of space wavered as if seen through rippled water, and a shiny metallic looking cylinder appeared.

Even as he moved the viewer towards it, the cylinder began its descent, and he had difficulty in keeping it in sight as it plunged down through the clouds and then hovered over the ocean below, a few metres above the sullen, almost still waters. A thick green mist sprayed out behind the cylinder as it began to move over the ocean, and it was only when some land appeared in one corner of the screen for comparison, that he realized just how big the cylinder was.

As there was little point in following the cylinder any further, he swung the viewer over to see how the waters were affected by the algae spray. The viewer dipped down below the surface of the murky ocean and Jed stepped up the magnification to a point where the individual cells of the algae could be seen. To his amazement, they had already begun to multiply in the nutrient rich water, tiny bubbles of oxygen indicating the carbon dioxide breakdown process had started.

It would be a long time before the process would have an overall planetary effect, allowing other species to mutate and develop to fill every niche available, but at least the stagnation of the planet was ended.

Jed went over to the wall mounted keyboard and screen, he felt in the mood to have another go at 'it', not that he expected to make much headway, but he had been awoken from his nap unexpectedly, and now he was awake it was worth a try.

After the opening pleasantries were completed, he began:

'Earlier you asked me for an assessment on a planet full of the most nightmarish creatures I have ever seen. Well, I have it ready.'

'Thank you. What do you think should be added or removed?'

'Frankly, nothing. It's doing rather well in my estimation. Everything is eating something else; every little niche has something in it, trying to survive. I particularly liked the fixed prongs on the creature by the fumarole, unable to take the smaller beetles, so allowing them to grow to maturity and keep everything in balance. Nice touch that.'

'Is there anything you think should be changed?'

'No. I think we should leave the planet alone. Perhaps we could have another look in a couple of millennia?'

'Is the last part of your answer a question or comment?'

'it's a suggestion. I think we should check it out again some time in the future.'

'Thank you. Your assessment of the planet and its life forms is correct.'

'That's most gracious of you, thanks a bunch.' Jed replied, thinking 'it' had been a bit condescending.

'Who or what is the bunch you wish to thank?'

'Forget it. It's just a saying we have. There is no bunch.'

'Then why do you refer to it?'

'As I said, it has no meaning, it's just something we say.'

'Why do you say things with no meaning?'

Jed had an uncomfortable feeling that he was being got at, and distracted from his real intent to give 'it' a hard time, so decided to change the subject.

'Why do you reply to me on the screen when the unit in my rest room and the enunciator talk directly to me?'

'Because that was how the first communication was initiated. Is it your wish that answers to your questions should be verbalized in future?'

'Yes please, I like to hear a voice, and then I don't feel so lonely.'

'The word lonely is not fully understood, please explain.'

'Who doesn't understand the word lonely?' Asked Jed hopefully, almost holding his breath.

'The word lonely means to be alone, without others of your type. The inference in your statement implies you do not like this. It is the dislike of this condition that is not understood.'

'Do you not sometimes want the company of others?' Jed thought putting the question in the negative might cause confusion, and thereby elicit an admittance of self from 'it'.

'Your concept of company has never arisen. It will be studied, and if there is a relevant answer to your question, you will be informed.'

Jed had hoped for some reference to 'I', 'Me', or anything to do with the 'first person singular', but he had been thwarted yet again by the ever vigilant 'it'.

His first idea was that 'it' was only a computer, albeit a very clever one, but somewhere at the back of his mind a little niggle existed, eluding to the possibility that there just might be a sentient being behind the scenes, and that intrigued him.

Thinking another approach might be a little more productive, he set about formulating another set of questions to try and get the information he wanted.

'Do I, and the complex, exist in the same time stream as the rest of the physical universe?'

'No.'

'Can you explain that please?'

'No. It is not relevant to what is being asked of you. Your knowledge of spatial physics is inadequate on that subject, you would find it difficult to understand the concept. This is a statement of fact, not a criticism of your ability or knowledge.'

'How do you know I wouldn't....'

'It is requested that this conversation be terminated. A situation has arisen which needs your attention. Will you comply?'

'I don't think I have any option, do I?'

'Will you comply?'

'Yes, I will comply, as you put it.'

The centre screen lit up showing a planet with a single land mass surrounded by water. The viewer swept down to within a few hundred metres of ground level, and Jed had a good view of the terrain, flora, and fauna, such as it was.

A coarse grass covered most of the open ground with a few stunted bushes poking up from the odd cluster of rocks. In the distance, a range of hills sat at the foot of a mountain range, the tops of its jagged black peaks clad in contrasting snow.

There was wildlife of sorts, mainly a variety of small four legged creatures, scurrying about cropping the rank looking grass and trying to dodge the attentions of a larger animal which seemed intent on converting their protein into fuel.

It was not doing very well, as the prey animals were fleeter of foot, and the predator lacked the necessary degree of cunning to compensate for this. This would be tricky to adjust.

Jed turned the viewer towards the sea, passing over a small desert area before returning to the ubiquitous grass plains, which made up most of the uninspiring terrain over which the viewer sped.

Although he had not observed a satellite, he thought one must be present, as the high and low water marks were quite obvious against the high cliffs where land met water, and that meant a tide system was present.

The thunder of gigantic waves against solid rock could be heard long before the viewer dipped down over the cliff edge to the raging ocean below. The first fifty metres of the turbulent waters were obscured from view by the spray mist, which billowed in huge clouds all along the coast for as far as Jed could see.

Taking the viewer below the surface of the tempestuous waters made Jed feel uneasy, although he knew he was not present himself, the reality of the scene was quite nerve racking.

There was little marine plant life close to the shoreline, but further out it flourished in great abundance until the sea bed ended in sheer underwater cliffs to the black abyss below.

Jed sent the viewer down until it reached a point where sunlight could not penetrate, and then the phosphorescent light of the frond like seaweeds and other strange plants clinging to the vertical cliff walls took over, bathing everything in an eerie pale yellow green glow.

At all levels he observed swimming creatures, in much greater variety and size than those he had seen on land.

He brought the viewer back up to the surface and went inland to check if there were different animal types further afield, but halfway across the single continent he found little change to those he had seen earlier, and assumed with good reason, the rest would be the same.

Jed thought the world was in a reasonably stable state, and said so via his keyboard, adding the lack of variety in land animal species could be corrected.

'Your assessment is accurate. Please suggest how you would increase land animal variety.'

Jed thought for a moment, and then remembered that on worlds where the land mass was broken into several separate units, each seemed to develop species most suitable to the prevailing conditions. This would also lessen the violence of the seas, which at present had three quarters of the planet to build up their waves in, before smashing into the land.

'If the continent could be split into several pieces and allowed to drift apart, then each section would develop its own specialist species to suit the different climatic conditions on each land mass.

Also, there would be more diverse ocean currents due to the channelling effect of the sub continents, and this would add to the climatic differences, and hence enhance species variation still further.

'There's only one problem, how do we slice the main continent into pieces?'

'Equipment for this can be supplied. What criteria would you use to decide where the incisions should be implemented?'

'Along any stress or fault lines. These would be natural break points for the continent, given enough time. The up thrust of the mountain ranges indicate there is plate movement down below somewhere, so once movement is started it should continue. Is there any means of detecting the fault zones?'

'Yes. The controls for this will be illuminated.'

The picture on the main screen changed to a flattened map view of the continent, and a touch pad began to softly blink.

Pale blue lines delineated the fault zones on the map as Jed worked the controls, and he wondered how this was achieved. Perhaps it was through the viewer? He would ask.

He studied the map intently, carefully selecting those fault lines which would break the continent into six independent pieces of varying shapes, and using the cross hair control, marked them for the splitting operation.

Jed wondered how the break-up of the continent would be

accomplished, and what mighty power source would be used. He longed to ask, but was not keen to be put down yet again for his lack of sufficient knowledge to understand the alien technology.

'It is assumed that you would like to witness the operation. When the equipment is in place you will be informed, and a brief description of the method used will be given.'

The screen dimmed to its normal quiescent state of a faint glow, indicating that work for the day was over, as far as 'it' was concerned. Jed had other things on his mind, and went up the tower lift to find isolation from what he felt was the stern and exacting atmosphere of the control room.

Leaning on the parapet, he gazed out across the plains and wondered how Tree was getting along. In a strange way, he had felt more at ease with Tree than he did with 'it', although 'it' had volunteered some information would be forthcoming as to how the continent splitting would be done, and that showed some understanding of his natural curiosity.

Each and every sunset seemed different, and Jed wondered how this could be as there was no weather system on the planet that he was aware of.

This time, the sky was laced with yellow and orange streamers, as if a feather had been dipped in the two colours, and lightly drawn across the almost purple horizon.

One thing Jed wanted to see was the loading and launching of organisms to another world. He realized he would have to wait until he was called upon to seed another planet with life forms, but doubted if he would be allowed to witness the process at take off point, somehow.

He had seen the loading and launch hall when first exploring the complex, but now he was restricted to the control room, rest room, and the viewing tower above.

The doorway out of the control room just did not exist anymore, despite frequent probing, and he wondered why he was no longer allowed to roam at will.

Jed would like to have visited Tree, as he felt an odd sort of kinship with the arborescent creature. He no longer thought of it as a plant once communication of a sort had been established, and it had imposed no restrictions on him except in the early days, and that was for his own good.

There was almost a crackle in the air as the sun's last lurid segment dropped out of sight below the horizon, and night rushed across Jed's world soaking up the last vestiges of light, leaving an impenetrable blackness, except for the diamond glitter of the stars.

Somewhere out there, he thought, is an ore ship, still aimlessly accelerating under full power, a planet full of people like him, some of whom waited patiently and in vain for his return, countless other worlds, populated with their own individual life forms waiting to be discovered, or even bypassed maybe, therefore never to have known anything other than themselves as they dwindled blissfully into extinction with the passage of time.

In the overall game of a mighty Universe, he, as an individual, mattered not one jot, or so he thought, but then things are not always quite what they seem.

The following day Jed was kept busy assessing three worlds which were not showing optimum progression, according to 'it'. The first two taxed him very little, but the last one proved a little more complex.

Ninety percent of its oceans were covered in deep pack ice, while the land was shrouded in glacial sheets many hundreds of metres thick.

Apart from a few patches of dark green water dotted with ice floes, and the thrusting brown peaks of several mountain ranges, it was a white world, reflecting most of the meagre light and heat from a distant sun back out into space.

The atmosphere was crystal clear, with no sign of a cloud or chance of precipitation, the water being locked up permanently in the vast ice coverings.

The planet's internal fires were at low ebb, as the continental plates were under no stress and were therefore not grinding against each other, providing molten magma for its extinct volcanoes to spew forth.

There was some life in the seas, but because of the ice encrustation, there was little opportunity for it to mutate into air breathing forms, and populate the land.

The only non aquatic life Jed found was on the bare mountain peaks, where small beetle-like creatures scurried about harvesting a tough grey green moss which reluctantly grew in small patches on the sunny side of the rocks, and there wasn't much of that.

The moss was only just able to sustain itself against the marauding beetles. Replacement growth was difficult as it was unable to extract enough nutrients from the glass hard rocks which refused to give up their mineral rich contents to the feeble rootlets of the struggling moss.

It only needed a small increase in the beetle population to wipe out the moss, and then the beetles would also perish.

If a little extra heat and carbon dioxide could be brought into the equation, and perhaps some means of releasing the nutrients locked up in the rocks, then the planet could be eased out of its torpor and new species would develop.

Jed checked the land mass for stress lines, and was disappointed to find none. As there were no tectonic plate strains to relieve, heat and carbon dioxide release from volcanic action was unlikely, and the amount of free water was insignificant and too cold for an algae bloom.

That only left the beetles and the moss, unless he introduced another species, and that could upset the overall balance in the future

Using what he thought was possibly a spectral analyser, he found there was plenty of carbon in the rocks in the form of various metallic carbonates. If these could be released, then he would have the gas he needed to warm the atmosphere, and an abundant food supply for the moss.

The only thing Jed could think of was a lichen, but it would have to be able to survive vigorously in a cold climate and die out as the planet warmed up so as not to compromise the existing life forms, such as they were.

It took him the rest of the day to finally reduce the immense selection in the specimen hall to just four, and he ran them through the simulator along with the rock data to make his final choice.

Jed's intention of relaying his suggestion of how to bring the planet out of its present dormant state was pre-empted by the enunciator, drawing his attention to the fact that the equipment for dividing the land mass on the single continent planet was about to go into action.

He quickly tapped in the lichen data, was told his suggestions were correct, thanked, and told to watch the main screen as things were about to happen.

The usual spatial distortion preceded the arrival of the cutting equipment, which then took up a stationary orbit above the planet. It was difficult to judge its size as there was nothing nearby to compare it with, but based on past experience, Jed thought it was probably very large.

A thin frail spider's web of struts unfurled from one end of the cylinder, expanding out to form the framework of a huge parabolic reflector.

From the centre of the dish shape, a covering of some tenuous shiny material drew itself along the struts until the whole framework was one gigantic mirror. The whole assembly then detached itself from the cylinder, drifted some distance away, and rotated until the weak light from the distant sun was gathered up and focused onto the end of the cylinder.

Jed waited for some time, expecting something spectacular to happen, when it did. A hair thin beam of energy lanced down to the planet below, striking the coastline of the continent and slowly tracing inland, following, Jed hoped, the pattern he had laid out earlier.

As the beam moved across the ground, it was followed by an upward racing wafer thin stream of steam and dust as the rocks below disintegrated, and turned into their constituent parts.

Jed had no idea how deep the beam penetrated, but once a section had been completed, a flaming bright line of lava exuded from the slit, spilling out over the ground like so much glowing red treacle.

He watched, fascinated, for some considerable time, but realized he would not see the actual movement of the separate sections of the continent, as this would take many years to accomplish, creeping sluggishly apart, far too slow for the eye to follow.

Before finishing for the day, Jed thought it might be a good time to ask if he could go down to the load and launch hall, to witness first hand what happened when a cargo was dispatched.

'That cannot be permitted. It would be detrimental to your well-being. You can observe the operation using a viewer if you wish, and the launch into space can be observed from the viewer situated in the tower.'

'I didn't know there was one in the tower,' Jed tapped back, 'can it be used to view any part of this planet?'

'Yes, except for a few restricted areas.'

'How will I know where they are?' asked Jed, seeing an opportunity coming up for a little probing.

'You will be denied access to them.'

'On who's authority?' There was no reply to that carefully engineered dig, but he had no intention of giving up just yet.

'Are you still there?'

'Your communications can always be received'

'That's not what I asked.'

'Your specific implied meaning of the question is meaningless. There is no point in pursuing it further.'

Jed paused for a moment, this as going to be more difficult than he had imagined, but if nothing else, he was persistent.

'Are you aware of Tree?'

'*Yes.*'

'Is Tree part of this complex, or you, or anything here?"

'*No.*'

'Do you and Tree communicate to me in the same way?"

'*No.*'

'Why won't you admit to just being a machine?'

There was no answer, and Jed felt the tete-a-tete had been concluded, as the main screen went blank.

As usual, he had been thwarted by what he thought of as a machine, and it rankled somewhat.

Several 'days' went by, most of the time being taken up assessing the needs of various planets which somehow lacked the urge to progress as 'it' thought they should. Jed wondered if all his tasks were genuine, or if his competence was still being tested on mock-ups designed by 'it'.

Either way, he enjoyed working out the different problems and looked forward to the day when he might be asked to seed a virgin planet, if such existed.

Finding where the viewer was stashed on the top of the tower proved easier said than done, but Jed hesitated from asking for explicit instructions as to its whereabouts, as he did not wish to demonstrate his ineptitude to the seemingly perfect 'it'. Then he had the horrible thought that perhaps 'it' was 'all seeing' as well. Something was keeping a close eye on things.

A languid hand idly placed on the parapet revealed the hidden viewer, and on closer inspection he could just about see the touch pad's gentle glow against the stronger background light of the sun. The screen rose up silently before him and then lit up, showing the sand plain immediately behind it.

The controls were very similar to those he had used before, and when he had mastered them fully, he set off to see just how large the edifice really was.

Sending the viewer forward at walking pace, so that he had some idea of distance proved frustrating as the complex seemed to go on for ever, so he increased the apparent travel velocity just to find if the structure had an end.

It did, but it was a long way away from where he actually was, and there was no way of accurately judging its exact size, not that it really mattered any more. He now knew the complex was very very big indeed, and then there were the subterranean levels.........

Having satisfied himself on the enormity of the complex, he turned his attention to finding Tree.

The viewer sped over the sandy plains; the sickening realism of the tri-dimensional screen causing Jed to remind himself several times that it was the viewer, and not he, that was moving.

There was no sign of Tree, but then he had no idea of how far he had travelled when using the transporter portals, so it could be half way around the planet for all he knew.

When the rift valley came into view, he followed along its almost vertical walls until he came to the bridging tube which he had crawled along to reach the other side.

With the aid of the viewer he was able to enter the other pipe, which had been sheered off close to the cliff face, and travel up it for some considerable distance, eventually coming to a vast underground chamber.

The faint ambient light within the chamber highlighted several smaller dark openings high up in the chamber walls, but the viewer refused to enter any of them, and he wondered why. Swinging the viewer downwards, he saw light glint off something on the bottom of the spherical cistern, and moved in closer to see what it was.

A mass of metallic looking crystals twinkled and appeared to move as the viewer glided above them, almost giving them the semblance of life. Jed thought they might be some form of catalyst, changing the quality of whatever fluid the chamber had held, but he had no idea of what that might have been.

The chamber was devoid of any other interesting features, so Jed guided the viewer out into the open air to continue his search for Tree, flying low over the foam lava fields which had proved so troublesome when he had attempted to cross them earlier on foot.

Jed took the viewer up a little higher to increase the scanning range, and he then saw the top of Tree in the far distance, like a grey green beacon on the honey coloured undulating sands of the desert.

When he had left Tree, it was big, and spreading out a little more each day, but now it was massive, and towered over the landscape, some two hundred metres in height.

The trunk had thickened to support the spread of huge limbs, most of which were twice his height in thickness, while the lesser branches sported a huge variety of strange things Tree had grown for its own unfathomable needs.

Jed felt an urge, an odd ache, to contact Tree again, but unable to leave the complex as yet, it just remained a strong desire which would remain with him for some time to come.

He sent the viewer in amongst the branches, marvelling at the weird looking growths Tree had produced and trying to guess their purpose, but deep down he hoped Tree would notice his presence, or at least that of the viewer. Then he remembered the viewer did not exactly exist in the real world as did other things, so the lack of response from Tree was hardly surprising.

Circling the viewer around the colossal trunk before returning to the complex, he saw something which made him blink in disbelief. Standing beside the towering trunk was a perfect replica of himself, complete in the space suit he had been wearing just before his body gave up the unequal struggle against the hostile environment of the planet, and it looked a good as new.

It looked so real he expected it to move at any moment, but when he looked closer he could see that it had been grown from the same kind of material that Tree was made of, and could never sustain life. But then, he had not accredited Tree with life, at first. Jed felt... He was unable to define it.

So Tree had erected a statue in his memory, or was there some other explanation for Tree's creation?

Jed could think of no other rational reason why Tree should go to the trouble of making a copy of his former self, but then Tree had its own particular way of doing things, and he had not always understood what lay behind its thinking.

Taking one last look at his former self, and suppressing an involuntary shudder, he withdrew the viewer and the screen went dead, retracting back into its former hiding place within the parapet.

Jed stayed there, leaning on the hard parapet, deep in thought long after the sun had gone down, hardly noticing the brilliant firework display of colours which preceded the coming night, or the slight chill in the air as darkness fell.

There was something about Tree he could not get out of his mind, a bond, an affinity, an almost wanting to do something for Tree. Yet, when he looked at it rationally, he owed Tree nothing.

He had given Tree life, Tree had in turn given him a body, but if he had fallen a few metres further away, neither of them would be alive now. So no one owed anyone anything, but the feeling would not go away.

As Jed ate his evening meal, he felt more lonely than he had ever done since landing on the planet, and eventually lay down to rest feeling thoroughly miserable.

That night he dreamt about Tree, the deep rift valley where the planet had split apart for some unaccountable reason, and then falling through the viewing screen to land in the scene he had just been watching, with no way back. It was not a good night's sleep.

It was a tired and disgruntled Jed who stumbled into the control room next day to be greeted by the strident mechanical voice of the enunciator.

'Good morning Jed. You wished to observe the loading of a transporter. The left-hand screen will give a good view of what takes place in the main launch hall. The viewer can be moved to any position within the hall, but not outside it.'

'Thank you' Jed replied, but not with his usual enthusiasm.

The screen came to life with the viewer high up in the vast dome of the launching hall.

This gave some indication of its overall size, as the 'spokes' radiating out along the ground from the base of the launch tube looked no thicker than so many pieces of thread, and Jed could well remember how he was dwarfed by them when he had visited the hall before his incarceration in the control section of the complex.

Bringing the viewer down in a sweeping arc towards the base of the main column caught him by surprise, as his stomach turned over due to the realism of the picture and the sensation that he was the 'viewer' and not the observer at the screen. He stopped the viewer twenty or so metres above the ground, and swung it around to face a section of wall where a conveyer strip extended out towards the main column.

The strip seemed to finish at the wall face, but Jed knew better, there would be an opening when the time was right, and he waited patiently for the lichen loaded containers to appear.

Some moments later a slight shimmer on the wall's surface announced the imminent arrival of a container, and when it came into sight on the extension of the conveyer, it was its sheer size which took him by surprise.

Twenty metres in diameter and over one hundred metres long, it slid silently along towards the central column, to be followed by another one a few metres behind. Jed watched in amazement as the conveyer slowly filled with cylinders, all progressing towards the main central column.

As the first cylinder drew near to the launching device, a section of the conveyor heaved the container upright, and it disappeared into the cavernous hold of the transporter.

Jed counted eighteen containers in all, and began to wonder just how large the actual transporter itself was.

One by one, the massive cables hanging down from the walls twitched, as power was fed into the copper coloured toroids which joined the spokes to the central column, a soundless hum, felt rather than heard, filled the huge dome of the launching hall, Jed found it difficult to understand how he could feel something which was being transmitted by a picture.

Soon all the toroids were glowing with an inner light and, due to the massive build up of power within, the air around them shimmered, and they appeared distorted to him. He knew the actual launch was very near.

Abandoning the viewing screen, Jed hurried into the rest room to use the tower lift, as he wanted to see the launch with his own eyes, not have it relayed to him by a screen, as realistic as it was.

Scanning across the vast flat top of the complex he could see no sign of activity, but then he had no idea where the transporter would emerge from, except knowing it would not be nearby as he would have heard something on earlier launches.

In the far distance the air shimmered for a moment, and then the transporter left the complex in a blur of movement almost too quick for the eye to follow.

As it streaked upwards, a faint vapour trail was left behind as the air pressure behind it dropped, the air rushing in to fill the space punched out of the atmosphere as it ascended, and causing what little water vapour the air held, to condense into a thin mist.

Eight:
Corrections

LIGHTNING SIZZLED AND crackled in the tortured column of air which extended to the fringes of space itself, and Jed clapped his hands over the holes in his head which served for ears, knowing full well that much air displacement was going to be accompanied by a large bang.

The transporter was now just a small shiny speck high overhead, only visible because of the sunlight which reflected from its metallic surface, and then there was the customary warping of space signified by the ripple effect of the distortion field, and it was gone from sight.

When the concussion wave arrived it rattled his bones and made him gasp for air, giving him a very good idea of just how much energy had been expended in a very short space of time.

Within seconds, all was peaceful and quiet again, the transporter well on it way across the galaxy to disperse its cargo of rock eating lichen onto a world which would never be quite the same again.

Jed was still trying to get the scale of the operation into some perspective, when the 'ping' of the enunciator broke him out of his reverie. He was needed down below, and so returned to the control room to see why.

'Do we have a problem?' Jed asked cheerfully, sitting down.

'No. A problem is whether to do something or not. A difficulty is how to do something. There is a distinct difference between the two words. You seem to have adopted a colloquial meaning for some of the words you use. That makes it difficult to extract your exact meaning when in communication with you.'

The voice was flat, as usual, with no intonation, and Jed could feel his hackles rising at what he considered to be a rather pedantic criticism of his ability to express himself.

'OK. Got what you said. Understood. I will try to be more careful in future,' he tapped in on his keyboard, glad that his actual feelings were filtered out by the intervening keys.

'What do you want me to do?'

'Two planets have been located which need your attention. Both are in the same solar system and have stabilized to a point where there is no further development of the indigenous species. It is preferable that no new species be introduced to correct this situation. The first planet is now on your screen.'

A few fluffy white clouds broke the otherwise clear atmosphere which surrounded the planet. There was no main land mass as such, only innumerable small islands, evenly dispersed in a dark blue green ocean. As the viewer swept lower it was evident that each island had developed its own type of vegetation, each subtlety different from its neighbour.

Jed brought the viewer down to ground level, and found a wide variety of creatures scampering about, some obviously carnivorous, while others chewed on the lush vegetation and fruiting bodies fallen from the clumps of tree like growths which dotted the flatter parts of the island.

Each island seemed to have a central peak or prominence, probably an extinct volcano which had brought the island into being in the first place.

It was difficult to be sure, as weathering had destroyed the telltale sharp edges of a possible cinder cone, and the copious covering of greenery hid any other details of what might have been.

Jed spent a considerable amount of time scanning the islands, but could find no fault which he thought should be corrected, as each Island had its own hierarchy of creatures, based on the same fundamental theme.

Jed had to withdraw the viewer out some distance from the planet to find its twin, circling around in the same orbit, but on the other side of the sun.

It was truly a twin, the same pattern of small islands dotted about on its ocean, and when he took the viewer in for a closer look, the wild life had developed in much the same way. Again, each island had its own particular variation on a basic theme, and that included the plants.

To be sure that all was well, he took the viewer down to see what the oceans had to offer, and caught sight of something floating in the water. A large tree trunk had been washed out to sea, with a small group of short four legged creatures clinging to its rough bark.

If the ocean currents were kind enough, he though the floating menagerie would finish up on a sandy shore somewhere, and add to the existing collection of wild life on that particular island.

At thirty metres below the slowly heaving waters, he levelled the viewer out and cruised along, noticing the different types of swimming creatures and trying to get some idea of which ate which.

A huge dark shape loomed out of the faintly cloudy waters, and he slowed the viewer down to prevent a collision, still having trouble with the concept that the viewer would pass through anything in its way, as it did not exist in the same space time continuum as that which it viewed.

The shape turned out to be a massive growth of seaweed, anchored to the ocean floor deep below by a single strand of what looked like rope.

Dipping down below the main mass of weed, Jed moved the viewer in closer to the anchor strand and then saw why it reminded him of rope. The anchor line was twisted into a helix, forming a natural spring.

Something was crawling up the strand from the depths below, and he followed it with the viewer to see if his suspicions were right. An almost white body equipped with many stubby legs made steady progress up towards the mass of weed above, tiny suckers holding the creature firmly onto the swaying strand as it rippled its way up.

As it approached the first clump of frond-like weed, a small shoal of swimmers left the sanctuary they had enjoyed, and sped off to the next clump above.

The white thing twisted the lower half of its body around the anchor strand, while the rest of it leaned out, the unused legs slowly transforming into a good imitation of the frond like weed above.

When Jed saw the head, he knew he had been right. A small mean slit of a mouth with two glistening black eyes above it, swung around, and looked directly into the viewer.

He suppressed a slight shudder, subconsciously thinking any movement on his part might provoke an attack, or frighten the creature away.

As there was nothing nearby with which he was familiar for comparison, he had no idea what size the creature was, but made a rough guess of about three metres, based on the troughs between the waves.

While he watched, the creature changed colour to match the weed above it, and before long would have disappeared from sight if he had not known where to look for it.

One by one, the little swimmers returned to their favourite hiding place in the weed, and the grasping fore limbs of the creature from the depths caught them, and passed them along to its slit-like mouth, ingesting them whole.

A quarter of the shoal had been spirited away before the rest of them realized what was happening, and the survivors turned tail and fled back to the weed clump above.

Further up in the green canopy of the weed, something sensed that a meal might be in the offing, and sent several exploratory feelers down to see what it was.

Thin grey and yellow mottled ribbons slithered downwards, touching and probing everything they were not familiar with until they came upon the creature from the depths, who was still looking for little swimmers.

Before it could retreat down the stem to safety in the dark waters below, the ribbons had wrapped themselves around several of its legs, despite the green camouflage.

The ribbons tightened, and a row of tiny teeth on the inside edge of the ribbons dug in deeply, severing five of the creature's legs and hauling them up into the mass of greenery above.

The creature from the depths discarded its camouflage and quickly transformed its remaining legs into their sucker form to begin its journey downwards, but it was too late. The severed legs were considered a delicacy by the one above, and thicker ribbons were speedily sent down, entwining around the now white body and neatly slicing it into manageable sections, which were then drawn up one by one to something Jed was unable to see.

The remaining shoal of little swimmers returned to their chosen home after a while, and began the breeding process to replace those who had been eaten.

Jed visited many other weed colonies, all of which seemed to have a similar types of life except for one, which specialized in a bizarre collection of crustaceans.

They all had exoskeletons of some kind. Some had thin, fragile, almost translucent shells, while others were heavily armoured and equipped with vicious looking pincers. Many looked like the weed they hid in, others blatantly coloured to warn off attackers, not that it made much difference.

To Jed, both worlds seemed to be doing very well, and as far as he was concerned, needed little, if any interference from him, or anyone else.

'I see no reason to interfere with either world, they are both doing well. There is some migration between the islands, and that should keep the species changing. It seems a little odd to me that both worlds should have similar life forms, can you explain this?'

'Both planets split off from their sun simultaneously, and therefore had identical physical conditions. An earlier seeding was done based purely on data received of those conditions, consequently they had the same starter implantations.'

'Do you mean that a sentient being wasn't involved in the selection?'

'Yes.'

'In other words, a computer or something similar made the choice?' There was a longer than usual pause before the answer came back.

'Yes. The implantation was based on data alone.'

'Is that why I am needed here, to add that little extra touch of finesse?'

'Please explain finesse.'

'it's a quality we humans alone have. You could say it's a subtlety of discrimination, a delicacy of judgement and execution. That little touch or alteration that turns something which is adequate, into something even more acceptable or possibly beautiful.'

'It is a quality possessed by sentient life forms for the enhancement of a necessity. That is now understood.'

'Is that why I was brought to this place, to add that little extra touch to the work carried on here?'

'You have assumed correctly.'

'Did you select me to come here?'

'No.'

'Then who did?'

'That information is not available.'

'Not available to you, or me?'

'The two questions you have asked cannot be answered in a form which you will understand. There is no point in pursuing the questions any further. It is considered that in time you will know the answers to these questions.'

'Can I ask you about this planet?'

'Yes. What do you wish to know?'

Jed thought he detected a slight change in tone, and wondered if 'it' was just a little relieved that the subject had been changed.

'The deep rift with the two pipes in it. What caused the rift, and what are the pipes for?'

'The rift occurred when the planet's outer surface shrank more than it's core. This is an unusual occurrence and the cause is unknown at this time. The pipes are part of a water supply system which was abandoned when no longer needed.'

'Who needed the water?' Jed asked, thinking he was about to unravel a few mysteries of the planet.

'*That is not known.*'

'Do you need water?'

'*No.*'

'Did the builders of the complex need the water?'

'*No.*'

'Then who did need it?'

'*That question has been answered.*'

'Not to my satisfaction, it hasn't.' He tapped in angrily. 'All right, how about the transporter portals?'

'*Your question is meaningless. Please rephrase.*'

'Who made and used the transporter portals?'

'*The builders.*'

'Who were the builders?'

'*Those who built the complex.*'

'Yes, but who were they?'

'*They are only known as the builders.*'

'Where did they come from?'

'*That is not known.*'

'Did they build you?'

'*No.*'

'Who built you?'

'*The question is meaningless.*'

Jed noticed the 'please rephrase' was omitted from the answer, and sensed that he would get no further in his quest for the speakers identity, at the moment.

'The pool where everything thrown in turns to liquid, what is it used for?'

'*Construction.*'

'Of what?'

'*Anything which needs to be constructed.*'

'This complex?'

'*The question is meaningless.*'

'Was material from the pool used to make this complex?'

'*Yes.*'

'How do you know that to be true?'

'*The information is in the data banks.*'

'Can I have direct access to the data banks?'

'*No. That is not permitted.*'

'If I tried to get access, who would stop me?'

'*You would be unable to gain access.*'

Jed was about to change the subject again in the hope of digging out the information he required, when he was interrupted.

'*With regard to the twin planets you gave advice on. Your assessment is correct, the planets will be left to develop naturally, but will be checked again in the future.*'

'Thanks for that. If you knew the answer, why did you ask me for advice?'

'*The data for and against interference was in balance, your assessment was required to make the final decision.*'

'Did you make the final decision?'

A longer pause than usual followed that carefully aimed dig, but this time 'it' changed the subject.

'*A large plasma cloud is approaching the planet. You may like to observe the effect it has on the atmosphere from the tower.*'

'Why do you think I might be interested in seeing it?'

'*You seem to be interested in the light displays at sunset.*'

'Is there anything you don't know about me?'

'*Yes.*'

'What do you wish to know?'

'*Why do you give an irrational response when being denied access to restricted information?*'

'it's something we humans call frustration, but I doubt you'll understand that.'

'*You are correct. An understanding of this phenomenon would be useful for future communications. The plasma cloud is about to make contact.*'

'OK, thanks. We'll talk again soon.'

Jed hurried over to the tower lift and jumped onto the platform.

As usual, Jed had no idea what time of day it was, so he felt little surprise when he saw the sun just about to sink below the horizon as the fringes of the plasma cloud brushed the planet's upper atmosphere.

A fine filigree of white and pale green light curved over the sky like a thin lace cap, deepening in colour as the heavier particles of the gas gave up their charge to the thin upper air.

Seconds later, clusters of vivid purple lines of light, as fine as the finest hair, curved downwards to the planet's surface, and Jed instinctively ducked as one such cluster came towards him, but it fizzled out long before it reached the ground.

A brilliant searing flash of lightning ripped down from high above, gouging out a small depression a mere five hundred metres from the edge of the complex, and sending up a little cloud of dust and sand as the charged atmosphere tried to rebalance itself.

The whole colourful display was suddenly obliterated by an intense pulse of pure white light which seemed to hit the planet with an almost physical force, and then it was gone, and so was Jed's vision.

He felt his body sway as a wave of giddiness swept through him, and he reached out for the cool firmness of the parapet to gain some stability. Jed's eyes slowly recovered, and he saw the white and green tracery of lights high above gradually fade as the plasma cloud moved on.

As his eyes got used to the velvet blackness, the stars came out again to light the heavens with their pinpoint diamond-like brilliance, and all seemed normal once more.

Jed wondered if Tree had faired well during the cosmic storm, but knowing Tree, if it had been struck by lightning, it would probably soak up the energy and tuck it away to put to good use later on.

Many days passed without any untoward incidents taking place, and Jed settled into the routine of assessing whatever planets the system brought to his attention. He now felt quite sure his judgement was being accepted without question, his probation period being well and truly over.

Although this placed much responsibility on his shoulders, he accepted it in the knowledge that he was becoming rather good at his job, and the temptation to be a little frivolous at times was held tightly under control.

He was still puzzled how the viewers worked, as the concept of something which did not exist in real time relaying a truly three dimensional picture back over an astronomical distance was beyond all his reasoning abilities. Slowly he came to terms with the fact that his was not the only science around, and just because his people had not discovered the principles involved, did not mean they were non-existent.

Tree often came into his thoughts, and he resolved to tackle 'it' about having a little time off to pay Tree a visit, not that he really expected to be let out of the control section of the complex, let alone onto the sand plains beyond.

One by one, with a little help and guidance from 'it', and as the need arose to use them in his work, he mastered the various devices around the walls of the control room.

One particular machine held him fascinated. He could watch it simulate the mutation of a plant or creature to suit the environment keyed in, thus testing its suitability for a particular project.

The fact that it looked so real, and took place in such a short time, never ceased to amaze him, and he longed to know what science lay behind the seemingly impossible. Jed began to experience a sense of purpose and general contentment he had never known before.

One thing Jed had given little thought to was his vulnerability to ageing, not that he felt old in any respect. His new body suited him very well, never tiring, not that he did much physical movement to cause it to feel tired.

He looked back on the days when he was travelling across the sand plains, and although he was impatient to reach his destination, or bored with the sameness of the terrain, he could not recall feeling exhausted at any time.

When the chance came up, he tackled 'it' on the subject.

'Is it known how long I will live for?'

'Please clarify the question.'

'Is it known when I will die?'

'You will never die.'

'You're joking, everyone dies sometime.'

'Jed, you are not using your past experiences to add data to your knowledge field. Please reassess the question. What do you really want to know?'

'Will I live for ever?'

'Yes.'

'But all people and animals...' and then it dawned on him.

'OK. Got it. I as a being, a unit of awareness, a whatever you want to call it, I will live on after the body I'm in breaks down and decays.'

'As it did on the sand plains, Jed. You recovered from that.'

'All right, how long can 'I' live for?'

'You are immortal. You have an infinite life span. Your kind are the only things in the universe which possess this feature.'

'But will I remember my past lives?'

'Do you remember your landing here?'

'Yes, who could forget that, but that's only one lifetime, what about the rest?'

'All memories are stored in your mind, and you mind goes with you from lifetime to lifetime. It is merely a matter of access. If you have

difficulty in recalling past lifetimes, it is possible that you are not meant to.'

'Why would anyone want to stop me from finding out about myself?'

'That is not known.'

'All right. How long will this body last?'

'A very long time relative to your idea of a lifetime.'

'Immortal?'

'Not quite. You also have the power and right to terminate the possession when you choose. The body has been designed to self repair and maintain itself for a very long time.'

'I thought Tree grew it for me.'

'That is correct.'

'But you implied …'

'Nothing is implied, only stated.'

'Is there some sort of link between you and Tree then?'

'Yes, but not in the sense you would understand.'

'I'm getting a bit fed up with this 'you wouldn't understand' bit, why wouldn't I understand?'

'You do not have the specific scientific knowledge to comprehend the principles on which this system works. This is not meant to demean your ability or qualities in any way, it is merely a statement of fact.'

'Could I acquire this knowledge?'

'Yes, that can be arranged at some time in the future.'

'All right, that's something I can look forward to then. Now, Can you explain why I am imprisoned in the control room?' The reply was so long in coming that Jed thought 'it' had gone off line.

'Jed, if you had the choice to remain here doing what you do, or return to your former life as if nothing had happened with no memory of this place, which would you choose?'

As he had never considered there was a choice, he had given it little thought before, but he did now.

'I would choose to stay. It is the most interesting thing I have ever done, nothing in the past can compare to this kind of work. Anyway, it's academic, I'm here now.'

Another long pause preceded the surprise answer.

'You are not held prisoner here. You are free to roam anywhere you like on the planet, except for certain areas where you might be in danger of damaging your body beyond repair. There are also certain sections of the complex to which you will not be allowed access for the same reason.'

'But there's no doorway out of this room, except to my rest room, so how the hell do I get out?'

'*The exit will now open for you when you desire to leave the control room. The passageway leading directly to the outside will be shown to you.*'

'Why was I not able to find the exit when I looked earlier?'

'*There was a reason. The reason no longer exists.*'

'Am I allowed to visit Tree when there's not much for me to do here?'

'*You may visit Tree whenever you wish. Your work here is not time constrained. It matters little when it is done.*'

'One other thing, I'm fed up with having to type everything on this bloody keyboard instead of being able to speak. Can I be fixed up with a larynx?'

'*It is physically possible. Please consult Tree.*'

'Do you know what I mean when I mention the dome?'

'*Yes.*'

'Can you answer questions about it?'

'*Some answers may be beyond your comprehension at this time, but in general, they will be answered.*'

'Is the dome a power generator?'

'*No. The dome is the cover for the power generator.*'

'OK smart arse, you got me again. You know bloody well what I meant. Am I correct in that the big disk at the bottom of the column is the main driving force?'

'*Yes, that is correct.*'

'Is it somehow coupled to the sun of this system?'

'*Yes.*'

'How is that done?'

'*The interspatial gravitational field of the sun is focused onto the base disk, locking it to the sun. As the planet turns on its axis, this provides the differential motion between the base disk and the rest of the column, which in effect, is part of the planet.*'

'The material the disk is made from, and why it alone is affected by the sun's gravity, is the bit you think I'll not be able to understand, I suppose.'

'*That is correct. The explanation belongs to the same field of science used in the construction and function of the viewers, and many other pieces of equipment here.*'

'Including the transportation portals?'

'*Yes. It is suggested you use these portals when you visit Tree.*'

'How will I know which direction to go in?'

'The portals will be pre set.'

'By you?'

'By the complex.'

'So you and the complex are not the same thing?'

'You are seeking data you will not be able to understand at this time.'

'Surely you can answer a simple question like that with a yes or no?'

'For the time being, please accept the fact that it is not as simple as you might think. In time, all your questions will be answered fully when the conditions are right.'

'You mean when I have understood the basics of this new science you use?'

'Yes. But it is not a new science. It is based on the same principles which brought this universe into being.'

'OK, you've made your point, I'll wait 'till later.'

It was two days later when Jed decided to visit Tree, and the exit from the control room appeared, as promised, when he approached the correct section of wall.

The passageway out of the complex a was a lot shorter than he had expected, and soon he was out on the familiar sand plain, and heading in the general direction of the first portal.

He was amused by the almost apologetic way 'it' had respectfully reminded him to take the food producer along on the journey, omitting to say he had not thought of it.

As the first portal came into sight, he had the same old feeling of apprehension as before about entering the strange device, but by the time he had passed through three of them, with the usual flicker of distorted space, the feeling was gone, and he felt quite blasé about using them.

Leaving the last portal, he somehow knew the rough direction in which Tree lay, and set off at a trot, the food producer bouncing about in its net bag as he pounded along.

The top of Tree came into sight long before he expected it to, it having grown even taller since he last saw it with the viewer, and there were still several kilometres to go before he would reach the colossal structure which now dominated the surrounding plain.

Despite not having done any real exercise for a long time, Jed found he was able to keep up the same pace for the entire journey, with no inclination to rest, although he was feeling the first pangs of hunger.

Now that the time had come, Jed felt a little uneasy about asking

Tree for a means of speech, remembering the unpleasant sensation last time he was swallowed up within Tree's mighty trunk to get his body modified.

As he crested the last rise before the ground levelled out to a flat plain, Tree came into full sight. It was now several hundreds of metres high, casting a vast dark shadow across the sands as though night was about to fall. The main trunk had developed a series of buttress like ridges to give extra stability and support to the massive growth above, and Jed wondered if it would ever stop growing.

Walking under the outer branches, he felt the heat of the sun drop away to a cool stillness, and the old feeling of being at one with Tree returned.

The branches were adorned with a multitude of pods, fluffy balls, clusters of spikes, and groups of petals which may have been flowers, although Jed thought perhaps not, as Tree would have no use for such, bearing in mind how the spores were blasted up into the air long ago.

He walked around the massive trunk in the cool gloom, marvelling at the precision with which Tree had spaced out the enormous buttresses, towering up into the canopy above.

Wondering exactly how he was going to get across the concept of speech in pictures, Jed leaned up against the trunk between two of the mighty buttresses. Pondering on the difficulty, he felt the trunk give way slightly behind him so that he was leaning back at an angle, although still on his feet.

Then came the sleepy feeling, and his eyes slammed shut.

Jed could see right out to the distant hills where a mountain range cut a dark jagged line across the horizon. Then he looked down to see the mass of Tree spread out below him.

'God, I'm out of my bloody body again!' He could hear the words ringing in his head. After the first pulse of fear had passed, he calmed down, as no harm had ever come to him before when he had been free of his body, and anyway, 'it', he felt sure, would be keeping an eye on things.

Was there a link, or even something stronger between Tree and 'it'? Was the whole complex somehow part of a planet wide entity which controlled everything here? Something was in charge, he was sure of that, but getting answers which made any sense was almost impossible.

He thought about the baubles Tree had decorated itself with, and he was down among them, but when he tried to leave the area around

Tree, he was unable to. There was no barrier he could see or sense, he just seemed to float out to the edge of the space Tree occupied, and could go no further.

Jed drifted among the massive branches for... he had no idea how long, looking at the many different things Tree had adorned itself with, and trying to work out what they were.

Suddenly, he was back in his body, standing with his back to Tree, and he turned just in time to see the trunk zipping itself up. At least, he had been spared the trauma of being 'born' again. Tree must be as all knowing as 'it', he thought.

The first thing he noticed was that his vision was not quite as sharp as it had been a few moments ago, not that it was poor, but it did seem to have lost a certain clarity. Apart from that he felt just the same, and began to walk out towards the brightly lit sands beyond Tree's shadow. It was good to feel the sun again, warming his back, but why should he feel cold? He felt quite warm before he lent against Tree.

'Perhaps Tree had to cool my body down to operate on it.' Jed thought, and then he remembered why he had come to see Tree in the first place.

His first attempts at speech were hardly recognizable to himself, let alone anyone else, and a degree of frustration welled up until he realized he would have to get used to using his new larynx as he had as a baby.

One by one the words became clearer, until he could string a sentence together, but by then it was almost sundown, and he knew he would have to stay the night in the vicinity of Tree, there not being enough time to get back to the complex before the black of night descended.

Standing there in the fading light, he looking up at his massive benefactor, he crossed his fingers and shouted,

'Thank you Tree, thank you very much.'

The tip of the branch nearest to him slowly bent down a few centimetres, returned to its normal position, and then repeated the action. So Tree could hear him, and understand what he said. If only Tree could talk back, perhaps he could get some answers to the questions 'it' always managed to evade, but then he dismissed the idea, realizing 'it' would probably put a stop to it before he had finished the question. Jed was about to look for a soft bit of sand to spend the night on, when he noticed a small but bright light slowly descending from high up in the branches. As it drew nearer, he moved forward, until it hung there, suspended on a fine thread at waist height.

It looked like a fine thin rod of some crystalline substance with a now fainter inner light, and as he put his hand out to touch it, the rod whipped around his wrist to form a complete circle, snapping off the thread with a faint 'ting' as it did so. It had happened so quickly, Jed had no opportunity to withdraw his arm, jump back, or perform any other evasive action. He now had a slim crystalline ring around his wrist, and wondered why Tree had done this.

'What is this for?' He asked, holding up his arm.

There was a rustle high up in the branches, the ring vibrated slightly, sending a faint tingle up his arm, and a long black spear like stick whistled through the air, burying its sharp end deeply into the sand, a few millimetres from his right foot. Jed realized that if it had struck his head, it would have probably killed him.

A hazy picture began to form in his head of the most hideous multi-fanged creature he had ever seen. As the picture became sharper, the head, with its fangs dripping saliva, turned around to look directly at him, and the crystalline bracelet sent a tingle up his arm. Now he knew what the bracelet was for. A warning device of possible danger, both animate and inanimate.

Whether this was on instructions from 'it' or just a gift from Tree, he had no way of telling, and did not like to ask. Jed set up his food producer, and after waiting the appropriate time removed the plum-like offering, savouring its delicate juices as they trickled down his throat. A good night's sleep under the stars, and he would be ready for the journey back to the complex.

Bidding farewell to Tree next day was not easy, as he could no longer give the trunk a good hug as he had done before due to its size, but he tried, as he could think of no other way to say goodbye. Somehow he felt a little foolish trying to wrap his inadequate arms around the mammoth growth, and as he stood back, the bracelet gave a barely audible 'ting',

Tree had accepted his message, and had responded.

Nine:
The End Game

SETTING OFF FOR the Complex, he loped along comfortably, thinking of what lay ahead now that he could speak. He realized a lot more practice would be needed before he became easily understood, and could well imagine 'it' taking every advantage of poor speech to avoid any awkward questions he might ask. This gave him the incentive to work doubly hard at perfecting his new art as he went along.

Jed thought he was in a direct line for the first portal, but suddenly he was in unfamiliar territory, the soft sand of the low dunes having given way to a coarse grit, which quickly turned to sharp stones. These were unpleasant to walk on, let alone run, and he decided to retrace his steps to see where he had gone wrong.

Leaving the sharp stone area was the easy part, as the finer gravel was self evident, but the gravel seemed to spread out in all directions, and his footprints on the way into the area were no longer visible. Jed headed for a small rise, and having climbed to the top, looked around for clues as to where the sand began. It was nowhere in sight.

Taking bearings from the sun was all very well in theory, but as the sun was approaching its zenith, it only gave a rough indication of the direction he wanted to travel in, but that was all he had to go on.

A shard field came into view about midday, every one of them a gleaming jet black. Rather than risk cutting himself on their razor sharp edges, he skirted the field, wondering what other uses they could be put to, apart from that which Tree had demonstrated.

A sharp rise in the ground ahead promised a viewpoint from which he thought he might be able to see something familiar, and he began the climb.

From the top of the hillock, Jed saw what he hoped was one of the portals. It looked more like a fabricated structure than one of nature's random happenings because of its clean vertical sides, but to reach it he would have to go down into a deep valley, the first he had seen on the planet, discounting the massive rift he had found long ago.

The descent was easy, the gravel having turned to the more normal mixture of sand and small stones which seemed to make up most of the planet's surface. The valley bottom bore the marks of a winding water course, smooth ovaloid pebbles lining the shallow gully which was now as dry as the rest of the surrounding area.

'So there was water here once upon a time,' he said out loud, practising his new speech making ability. 'And therefore plenty of vegetation.' He looked around to see if any of it had survived in a dehydrated form, but nothing remained of what was once a lush garden of strange alien plants, decorating the valley floor and slopes.

A scree slope of small loose stones and gravel barred his way out, so Jed walked along the dry stream bed, looking for a more suitable way up. A few hundred metres further on a bend in the deepening valley brought a change. The sides were much steeper now, and one section looked as if some mighty machine had sheared away the rock to form a smooth vertical slab, reaching right up to the plain above.

Along the base of the rock cliff, several dark holes suggested caves of some kind, and Jed went forward to investigate, as they looked as if they had been cleanly cut into the solid rock, rather than water worn or a natural faulting in the strata. The first cave was a square cut hole, going back into the cliff some ten metres or so, and empty except for some stones and sand which had drifted in.

The second cave was a little larger, and went back into the cliff even further than the first one. In the dim light at the back, Jed could just make out what looked like various pieces of metal, some twisted into grotesque shapes as if some powerful hand had wrenched them from some structure, and vented its fury on them.

Something white caught his attention as he was about to leave the cave, and rather than pick it up, not knowing what it was, he gave it a good kick, sending it rattling along the ground almost to the exit.

In the brighter light of the cave mouth, there was no mistaking the bone, and he walked around it several times before picking it up.

The bone had rounded ends, and was longer than any in Jed's old body, which left him wondering just how big its owner had been. Going back into the cave, Jed let his eyes get used to the dim light for a few moments before looking for more bones. There were plenty, scattered about as if whoever had once owned them had exploded, or had been systematically scattered by an angry adversary.

Because of the low light level, it was difficult to see if the bones belonged to more than one creature, and there were too many of them to make it a viable proposition to kick them all out into the open for further inspection.

Jed left the cave and headed for the next opening, when the bangle on his wrist gave a little tingle. He stopped in mid stride, looking around to see if anything posed a threat, but nothing moved, and there was no sign of hostility from the sombre looking dark rocks which surrounded him.

'Perhaps I just imagined it,' he said out loud, his voice coming back in multiple echoes from the enclosing rock walls. 'I don't see anything here to worry about.'

The next two caves contained much the same as the second one Jed had entered, the remains of something scattered about through total destruction, and each cave had its share of twisted metal fragments to accompany the dismembered bones.

To try and figure out what the metal belonged to, he dragged several pieces out into the open, but they had been so distorted by the ferocity of the attack, that what remained bore little resemblance to its original form, except a two metre long heavy gauge metal tube, and that had been snapped in two.

His first thought was that it had been a barrel from a gun, but there were none of the other features he would have expected to find from such a weapon. Leaving the metal debris at the cave entrance, he moved on towards the next cave, determined to solve the mystery. The bangle gave another little tingle, as if saying something was not quite right here, but was unable to pin point exactly what it was.

Jed flattened himself against the wall of rock, finding a narrow crevice to hide most of his body from whatever was out there, but all was still and silent.

This was one time Jed wished he could exteriorise out of his body for an unobservable look around, but as yet he did not have that ability.

Cautiously he looked out from his hiding place, and glanced up and down the valley. He could see nothing threatening, just rock, sand, and the water worn pebbles where a stream had once freely run.

If there was a threat out there, he would have to flush it out and deal with it in order to get safely out of the valley himself. A good sized stone lay at his feet, so he picked it up, and began looking for the ideal place to throw it.

Just in case whatever it was lurked in the next cave, he threw the stone across the valley, hitting the far wall with a resounding crack. The stone shattered into several smaller pieces, which in turn rattled around on the valley floor.

A pencil thin beam of light lanced out from the area of the next cave, and a section of the valley wall where the stone had hit was vaporized into fine dust, accompanied by a sharp crackling sound. Jed immediately squeezed himself back into the crevice, wondering what to do next.

There were very few options open to him. He could take a chance and sprint back up the way he had come, but then whatever it was might come out from its hiding place, and he would be exposed long before he could reach the bend in the valley. Perhaps if he threw enough stones it might run out of ammunition, but there were not that many stones within reach, and he would not be fooled by such a simple subterfuge, so it was unlikely that his adversary would be.

The only other option he could think of was to wait until darkness covered the land and then sneak back up the valley, but what if it had night vision? He carefully picked up another stone and threw it further down the valley. The light beam caught it in full flight, leaving just a puff of dust to slowly drift down the valley, dispersing in the still air.

Whatever it was, it was getting better at what it did, while he was running out of bait and patience.

Jed thought of many words to sum up the situation he was in, but did not dare vocalize any of them, as much as he would have liked to.

The next time he reached out for a stone, the bangle gave his arm a sharp reminder that something out there was not too friendly towards him, so he withdrew back into his niche in the wall to try applying a little reason to the situation.

Jed realized that he needed to see down the valley and locate the exact position of the 'whatever with the laser weapon', and for that he needed a mirror or something shiny.

The previous cave was only a short distance back up the valley and may contain something among the debris which would act as a mirror. Did he dare make a run for it? He could in theory, stay here indefinitely as he had the food producer in the net bag, but the prospect of that held little appeal to him.

Should he sprint for the cave, possibly making enough noise to attract a pulse of laser fire, or creep along quietly, hoping he would not be in the direct line of sight of the laser wielding menace?

Jed chose the quiet method, moving slowly and placing each foot down on clear ground lest a vagrant stone should rattle. The temptation to dash the last few metres to the cave was almost overwhelming, but he resisted, and that probably saved his life.

Although safely in the cave, any noise on this silent world might elicit a response, so he picked up each piece of metal as if it were made of the finest fragile china, until he came to a really shiny piece on the end of a section of square rod.

He could not imagine what it had been part of before disassembly took place, perhaps the previous owner also needed to look around corners, but then it was far more likely it just happened to have the properties he needed and was really nothing to do with covert viewing.

Going to the cave mouth, he pushed the mirrored rod slowly out as far as it would go, and then manoeuvred it around carefully to get a good view of the series of caves down the valley. There was no sign of movement, so another stone was needed to get some action.

After propping the mirror in such a position that he could look down to observe the results of the exercise, Jed threw the stone as high as possible, so that it would arc down in front of the cave, disguising its point of origin.

As predicted, the laser beam disintegrated the stone just before it hit the ground, the puff of dust clearly indicating the opening from which the laser had been fired. Now he knew where his advisory lay, but what to do about it?

Turning the mirror rod around, he was able to look up at the rock face above the cave, and noticed that it was not quite as featureless as he had first thought. A few metres above the cave he was in, what looked like a small ledge ran along above the cave system.

If he could get up there, perhaps he could circumnavigate the caves, returning to the valley floor well past them. There were many fine cracks and grooves on the almost sheer surface, but they were far too narrow to get his fingers into, and then he trod on a piece of metal.

Selecting pieces of debris which were thin enough to be pushed into the cracks, Jed very carefully began to build a stairway of metal pegs up the rock face.

It took a long time, with many journeys climbing up and down the pegs, and much patience, but eventually he reached the ledge above the cave. After so much effort, he was relieved to find it was just wide enough for him to traverse along, taking him above the line of caves, but it petered out just before he was able to clear the last one.

In desperation he looked around, hoping for a miracle, and found one just above his head. A large piece of rock jutted out from the cliff face, and because of the nature of the cliff, he knew it must have broken away and be lying on another ledge like the one he was on.

The prospect of climbing down again for more pegs was daunting, but there seemed little option. After selecting enough pegs to reach the next ledge, Jed looked around for a stout piece of metal to prise free a supply of missiles from the cliff, he wanted to get the laser user out into the open so that he could see what he was up against.

While placing his new supply of pegs in the cliff face, one slipped from his grasp and fell spinning to the ground below.

A brilliant flash of light as the metal was vaporized, rammed home the point that a mistake now would be fatal.

Jed placed the metal rod on the ledge above, and heaved himself up after it to find the ledge was much wider than he could have hoped for. If he stood back against the cliff face, he would be out of sight unless his adversary advanced out halfway across the valley floor, and he would be totally concealed if he crouched down behind the loose rock on the lip of the ledge.

Suddenly he felt safer, and sat with his back to the cliff, planning his next move. Where the ledge finished, there were enough loose stones and small pieces of rock to entertain the laser for some considerable time, but would it run out of power before he ran out of ammunition?

Jed's attention kept going back to the big loose rock on the ledge. If he could get his adversary to stand directly below, he might be able to lever the rock off the ledge and splatter it all over the valley floor.

Even if he could get it out into the open, his chance of getting a direct hit was small, and the falling rock could easily be side stepped.

He needed to get it rattled, engage its attention fully, and then drop the rock. With luck, it would fire at the descending rock, converting it into a multiple barrage of stones.

Jed liked the idea of the rock being smashed into many pieces, as this would increase his chance of getting a direct hit, whereas a single missile could be avoided. He just hoped the laser was not powerful enough to vaporize his missile instead of shattering it.

Using the metal rod, he was just able to ease the rock to the very edge of the drop, where one final heave with the lever would send it on its way down. Next, he had to get his adversary out in the open, and a little angry if possible.

Jed piled the loose rocks and stones from the end of the ledge behind the big rock, and began to drop them in front of the cave below. The first few were hit with unerring accuracy, but nothing ventured out to see where they were coming from.

His pile of ammunition was being depleted without the necessary response, and then he tried dropping them beside the cave entrance so that they made a noise, but were out of direct sight of the occupant.

At first, just the bright metallic end of the laser came into view, and then he tried dropping two rocks at a time, one each side of the opening. Jed was not prepared for what emerged from the cave below.

A hunched up four legged creature with the laser clasped in its forearms rattled out into the open, swinging the weapon up and down the valley, looking for a target.

What shocked Jed motionless was not the size of it, for it would have towered over him by some four metres if he had been down there, but its composition. It was a moving skeleton, a collection of bones without a covering of any kind. A massive oval skull swung to and fro, looking for the stone thrower, while the long multi-jointed arms holding the laser unit tracked the head movements in anticipation.

Such creatures belonged to nightmares, although Jed could not recall having seen one quite as horrific as this, and he shuddered at the thought of confronting it at ground level.

With the lever rod in place, he leaned over the ledge, throwing one last stone aimed at the monstrosity, and yelling a string of obscenities at the top of his voice.

It produced the desired effect. The great skull swivelled upwards, the laser tracking its movements exactly and Jed put all his weight on the lever.

With a grinding sound, the huge rock teetered on the edge for a moment, and then accelerated down towards the hideous animated collection of bones below. The sharp crackle of laser fire echoed crisply back from the valley walls, to be quickly followed by a thunderous crack as the rock disintegrated under the impact of so much heat, and the now shattered rock rained down on the laser toting skeleton.

Although the fragments were only ten to twenty kilos each, there were many of them, and their combined mass was just the same as before the rock was hit.

Many bounced off the larger bones, but some found weaknesses in the structure, and slowly the warrior skeleton began to disintegrate as many linking bones were either snapped or dislodged from their joints.

To Jed's horror, the crumbling monster still tried to bring the laser to bear on the ledge, and the random firing of the deadly weapon blew chips of rock off the cliff above, showering him with the hot debris.

There was one large stone left on the ledge, and Jed grunted as he lifted it up. Taking careful aim, he launched it at the still gyrating skull below. Unfortunately it missed its target, but the end result was the same as the heavy stone severed the spinal connection to the head, and it lay still at last.

Apart from the odd twitch from a few main bones which were still joined, the skeleton creature lay inoperative, its laser weapon still clasped in its severed bony hand, but no longer emitting the deadly rays.

No other creatures had come storming out of the caves to its rescue, so Jed assumed that it was a lone operative, left over from a time long gone when the valley had something worth protecting.

He began the long climb down to the valley floor, leaving the metal climbing pegs in situ, as he saw no point in reclaiming them for further use, hoping to find a less arduous means of regaining the sand plains above.

Jed could not resist a close inspection of the scattered remains of the skeleton, as he suspected it had not always been such a bony apparition.

As he approached the remains, he waved his bangled arm out in front as he walked, waiting for the tell tale tingle which would warn him of impending danger, but there was no response from the magic bangle.

The skull seemed to be the most obvious choice for the control centre, and to a degree he was right. It contained a mass of crystalline blocks which must have been its sensors for vision and sound.

Set deep within the two eye sockets, a single crystal of some dark substance glared balefully out at him, some small vestige of energy lingering within its inky depths, and still trying to perform its intended function.

The main control centre of the creature was located within a now split open hollow bony structure set deep inside the chest cavity, and protected from outward assault by the massive ribcage. A stone must have fortuitously passed between the ribs to have dealt the fatal blow.

There were no obvious means of how the creature obtained its motive power, or transmitted control messages from the centre within its chest. Jed assumed it must have been done through the actual bones themselves, but when he tried to break one of the larger leg bones to see what was inside, he was unable to, no matter how hard he struck it against a rock.

He thought it more than likely the creature was once covered in some kind of skin to make it look more like a living entity, but any vestige of covering had long since disappeared, leaving him to speculate on what the whole assembly would have looked like, apart from darn right terrifying.

As the other two caves contained the broken remains of similar monstrosities, he wondered what their attackers must have been like, and what weapons they had used to overcome the incumbents.

Jed thought the laser might come in useful at some time in the future, and so tried to prise it free from the steely grip of the skeletal hand with its still attached arm. Even using the lever rod, he only managed to snap two fingers off, and then discovered it was an integral part of the creature.

He toyed with the idea of taking the whole thing, but then was unable to locate a firing button or trigger, so assumed the signal to fire must have come from the main controls within the chest.

There was nothing more to be gained from the dismembered guardian, so he walked on down the valley, passing several more empty caves, but no skeletons, or even the remains of them.

The cliffs either side had closed in now, the valley becoming more like a slit in the planet's surface with high unclimbable walls towering above.

Jed was contemplating whether he should return up the valley and see if there was another way out, when the bangle on his wrist tingled, warning him that something in the vicinity was harmful. He scanned the dark and sombre cliffs on either side for loose rock, and the valley floor for movement, but all was still. There were no caves for anything to hide in, and the ground was smooth and even.

Jed stepped back a few paces, and the tingling stopped. Why was the valley floor so smooth and free from debris?

He would have expected to see some small stones, or even a rock or two, fallen from the cliffs above, but there were none, just smooth sand, and that somehow felt wrong.

Picking up a roundish stone, he bowled it, like a ball, along the ground where he had been about to walk. The stone rolled along, as stones do, and then disappeared.

He picked up another one, and this time watched it very carefully. About five metres from where he was standing, the stone sank into the sand, as did several others which followed it. One stone, thrown a little to one side of the others, remained on the surface, so he threw a few more and soon had a safe pathway marked out for about ten metres, not that he felt inclined to try walking on it just yet.

So this was the second line of defence to protect something which probably no longer existed, or did it? He approached the first stone which had remained on the surface, and the bangle gave a slight signal to his wrist. Shuffling forward, to leave a distinct mark where it was safe to tread, Jed advanced to the second stone.

When he swung his foot over to one side of the marked pathway, the bangle reacted instantly, giving him a nasty shock right up his arm. Slowly he advanced along the line of stones until he came to the last one, and then stopped.

As he still had the lever rod, it was only a matter of probing the ground ahead to find where it would support him, but as he progressed down the valley, the safe path took on a twisted nature, weaving from side to side, so that unless the path was marked, there would be little chance of reaching the other end, wherever that was.

A slight deviation from the probed path brought a sharp reminder of the danger, and Jed wondered why he was risking his life just to see where the path might lead.

A few more metres and he was back on solid ground, but he still tapped the way ahead for a while, just to be sure.

The cliffs were almost touching overhead now, and what little light which managed to filter down was only just adequate for him to see his way, so he almost missed the massive portal carved out of the living rock, until he was about to enter it.

Jed thrust his arm into the opening, hoping the bangle would forewarn him of any dangers, but there was no tingle, only a glowing light from the amulet. He took two steps into the darkness, and the bangle increased its light output considerably so that he had to place his other hand between the bangle and his head to block out the intense light.

He was standing in a large cavern, cut out from the rock as the walls were so smooth and symmetrical. Two dark openings in the opposite wall led further into the rock, each with a symbol above it, but they were meaningless.

His natural instinct was to explore the tunnels, and with the aid of the bangle to warn of any danger, and its brilliant light to guide him, he thought it reasonably safe to do so.

As it was directly in front of him, Jed chose the left-hand tunnel, and was surprised to find how big it was as he drew nearer to its black opening.

The slap slap of his feet echoed back with a hollow sound as he walked along the tunnel, checking the side walls for anything interesting or that might pose a threat.

He had only gone some few hundred metres when the light from the bangle illuminated a side cave, and he cautiously waved his bangled arm in its opening to see what it contained.

The light reflected off a huge block of what he thought must be glass, because he could see a dark shape within its confines, but the details were obscured by the light refracting and reflecting back and forth from the transparent cube.

Jed drew nearer and then stopped in mid stride as the contents of the cube became apparent. Glaring out from its glassy prison was another guardian of the valley, only this one had its full covering of skin.

So far, the bangle had given no warning of danger, so putting his trust in Tree's gift, he moved forward, despite the natural urge to run. Jed tapped the glass structure with his knuckles, and then the bangle. It seemed to be hard and solid, with no apparent joins at the corners, but he could not discern its thickness, hoping it was adequate in case the creature inside suddenly came to life.

Jed had already concluded from his inspection of the remains back in the valley that the creatures were purely mechanical devices, but the realism with which they had been constructed still sent a shiver down his back.

He was very careful not to touch anything which might activate the 'guardian', not that there was much else in the great cavern, apart from some square box-like objects off to one side of the transparent cage. Jed walked around the block, marvelling at the hideous construction it contained, and wondering why the makers had chosen to use an animal form to defend their domain, instead of just plain weaponry.

He thought perhaps they were the interlopers here, collecting or mining something which the natural inhabitants were reluctant to lose, or maybe they just resented strangers in their world. The sand trap at the entrance to the cavern was, in his opinion, rather crude, although effective, but why not just have a big reinforced door?

He left the cavern with the spare guardian squatting forlornly in its cage, and continued along the tunnel, but not for long. Ahead was a door of huge proportions, blocking the tunnel with a finality that even Jed could sense.

Made of some shiny metal, it sat squat and defiant, a series of large studs protruding from its surface, bonding the outer face to something much stronger behind.

A recessed square panel, decorated with a collection of symbols invited Jed's fingers to touch them, but as he reached forward to try a random selection, the bangle warned him not to. He tried a second time, and again he felt the tingle, so he decided to leave the door alone as it was likely that it had some self defence mechanism just waiting to be triggered into action.

Something had decided he was not a bona fide member of the inhabitants of the cavern, and was quite prepared to remind him of that fact should he try his luck with the door.

Returning to the main entrance, Jed went up the second tunnel, a little more warily this time, especially when he came to another cavern after only a short distance.

He advanced his arm into the opening, and the blackness of the cavern was transformed into a glittering light show as the radiance from the bangle was reflected back from hundreds of sparkling water clear shards.

'So this is what they were after.' Jed said out loud, his words returning in a series of multiple echoes.

The floor of the cavern was covered in neatly regimented rows of shards, which somehow gathered up the light from the bangle and sent it forth again from their sparkling tips.

Jed knew they were only crystalline lumps of mineral and therefore devoid of life, but he felt a strange sadness for them, locked away down here in the darkness.

He turned, about to leave the cavern, when he felt the urge to touch one of the shards. Not knowing quite why he did it, Jed stooped down and let the bangle come in contact with the tip of the nearest shard.

The effect was electrifying, all the shards glowed with an inner fire, light pouring from their tips and lighting up the cavern like daylight, while the light from the bangle dimmed, as if power was being drained from it.

The bangle's light output returned to normal, and Jed felt he had done something which was right, something good, although he was at a loss to explain it.

It now seemed all right to leave the cavern of shards, and he returned to his exploration of the tunnel. A few hundred metres further on and the tunnel ended as had the other one, with a very solid door blocking his way. It was identical to the previous one, and as much as he wanted to see what was on the other side of it, he let discretion be the better part of valour, and left the symbol pad alone.

As he returned to the main entrance, the shard cavern was still ablaze with light, much of it spilling out into the tunnel, which he had not noticed when he had left it earlier.

Were the shards extracting energy from somewhere else now that they had been brought to life by the bangle?

He hastened along, sensing that something was about to happen, and if it involved a large discharge of energy, he would rather not be in the vicinity when it did.

Approaching the main entrance with its massive columns, the light output of the bangle began to lessen, but not before Jed noticed a small recess tucked away beside the left-hand column.

If it had steps cut into it, he would have considered it to be a spiral stairway, but it was just a smooth slope, curving around upon itself until it disappeared into the gloom above.

At the base of the slope, a wedge shaped solid platform sat, a perfect fit for the sloping passageway, and then he realized what it might be. Jed looked for a cable or other means of hauling the wedge up the slope, but there was no sign of anything attached to the wedge, and the floor of the passage was as smooth as glass.

He expected to find some sort of control or touch pad on the nearby wall, but there was nothing. A close inspection of the wedge itself revealed a small raised bump on its back edge, and he gingerly reached in and pushed it with his hand.

There was no reaction from the wedge or anything else, no whine of a motor or hiss of compressed air, so he assumed the power was off, which was not unlikely considering the age of the installation.

The spiralling passage led upwards, which was what he needed to reach the plains above, also it was on the opposite side of the valley from which he had come originally. It was just a matter of climbing, he thought, but what if there was no exit?

Jed stepped onto the platform and gave the raised section a good push with his foot, just in case the extra pressure would activate the mechanism, but the block remained where it was, and a long climb up seemed the only option.

The glow from the bangle brightened as the ambient light of the entrance hall faded, and he began the long climb.

To begin with, his feet gripped the sloping surface quite well, but as he ascended the long spiral, more fine dust seemed to have accumulated through the ages, and if there had been any wind, it had failed to dislodge it.

Several times he had slipped back a few paces, only saving himself from an ever accelerating descent by pressing with both hands against the smooth walls until his feet could establish a grip on the dusty ramp.

It was difficult to determine how high he had climbed, but it felt as though it must have exceeded the height of the cliff by some fifty percent, when a faint glimmer of light from above renewed his hopes. Every step was now a potential danger, as the fine dust had the lubricating qualities of grease, and he had to wedge himself against the walls while he cleared the dust from the ramp with his feet before going forward.

Slowly the light above brightened, and Jed heaved a sigh of relief as he poked his head over the thin ragged wall of the shattered lookout tower. Below him was the plain, and in the far distance a small bump on the horizon was probably the transport portal, but it was too far away to be certain.

He turned his head to look down into the valley, and for a moment vertigo threatened his grip on the tower wall.

The spiral ramp had been cut out of the cliff in such a manner that its outer edge was only just within the boundaries of the surface, the wall itself being only a few millimetres thick on the valley side.

Quickly he turned his head back again towards the plain to see how far above it he was, and realized it was much too far to jump, besides which, a jumble of debris formed a neat collar around the base and he would have broken every bone in his body if he had landed on it.

More unnerving than the drop to the plain below, was the thinness of the tower walls. They were as smooth on the outside as they were internally, so there was no way he could get a grip on the slick surface to climb down.

It was only a matter of ten metres to ground level, but it might just have well been two hundred as far as Jed was concerned. He baulked at the idea of sliding down the ramp to the valley floor again, and looked around in desperation for some means of escape.

He could feel his arm and shoulder muscles tightening as he grimly hung onto the top of the tower wall, fearful of his feet loosing their grip on the slippery ramp, and him flying out at the bottom of the spiral like a cork out of a bottle.

Out of desperation, ideas are born, and Jed was desperate. Despite the thinness of the tower walls, he reasoned they must have been strong enough when built to serve their purpose. Maybe they had lost a little of their strength by now? He wedged himself against the central column and hit the top of the wall with the heel of his hand.

A small crack appeared running vertically downwards before turning back on itself, and he knew he could break a section of the wall out if he tried. Trying to work out how long it would take him to break the tower down to just above ground level soon put paid to that idea, but what if he could smash his way out lower down?

Two more thumps on the wall, and he had a sizeable chunk of stone like material to use as a hammer, but how would he know when he had reached the correct position in the tower to begin his demolition work?

Jed carefully estimated the drop in height with one complete turn in the spiral passage, and divided that into his best guess of his height above ground.

By leaving a mark in the dust to denote each complete turn of the spiral, he could count the turns going down, and with a bit of luck arrive at the right position to make his bid for freedom.

The first few turns were the worst, as the light faded and the bangle slowly increased its light output to compensate. As he descended, Jed grew more confident with his plan, and having arrived at what he estimated to be the right spot, began hitting the wall with all the force he dared, commensurate with stopping his body from beginning a slide to oblivion.

At first he was unable to make much impression on the tough wall, but as his hammer stone began to grow smaller as chips flew off it, a small hole appeared in the tower. Jed blew away the dust and put his eye to the hole. He was rewarded with a clear view across the valley to the plain beyond. He was out of position by half a turn.

'Not too bad,' he said out loud, mainly just to hear a voice again after so long. 'Now let's try the other side.'

When the hole was big enough for him to get his head through, he felt more than pleased with himself, it was only a drop of two metres at the most, and he felt sure he could cope with that.

By the time he had enlarged the opening enough to squeeze through, the hammer was reduced to a mere shadow of its former self, and he let it drop gently to join the rest of the broken wall below.

Minutes later, Jed was on the sandy plain and heading off in the direction of the transport portal, but evening overtook him, and he had to find a suitable place to set his food producer down for the last meal of a long and tiring day, and a soft spot to spend the night.

Next morning, as the sun eased itself over the horizon with its customary display of light streamers, Jed was feeling pleased with himself. He had overcome all obstacles in his path by the application of logic and a little cunning, and he wondered if 'it' would have approved of his efforts.

For the first time since his new-found freedom, he was looking forward to returning to the complex and his work, not that he had seen enough of the strange things the planet had to offer, but a mixture of exploration and a fascinating and fulfilling job was more than most people he had known could only dream of.

With the food producer back in its net bag, he set off again for the portal, but it was high noon before it came clearly into sight due to a few diversions he had to make to avoid a shard field and another deep scar in the planet's surface.

Jed arrived back at the complex having used an extra portal to those he had travelled through on his way out to Tree, and he wondered if 'it' had somehow been watching him and programmed the other portal into the sequence to bring him safely back. He would find out.

As Jed approached the complex, he could see no sign of an entry point, the smooth unblemished walls of the edifice stretched off to each side into the far distance. Two metres from the gleaming wall, and the door was suddenly there to welcome him.

In a matter of minutes he was back in the control room, and had flopped down in his seat.

'*Welcome home Jed. It is hoped you had a pleasant journey, and enjoyed your visit to Tree.*'

'Yes thanks. Oh, and thank you for linking in the extra portal, it saved me a long walk.'

There was no reply.

'Why don't you answer me?'

'*There has been no question, only a comment. A comment does not normally require a reply.*'

'OK, did you link in the extra portal?'

'*No, it was done automatically for your convenience.*'

'Thanks anyway. Do you know about the mechanical monster guarding the valley I had to cross, and the underground facility at the valley's end?'

'*Yes.*'

'OK, what can you tell me about them?'

'*The underground facility was constructed by a visiting race who were harvesting the pulse crystals.*'

'You mean the shards.' Jed interrupted.

'That is the name you have assigned to them.

'The indigenous race on the planet objected to their removal on religious grounds, and attempted to stop them. The mechanical guardians were installed to prevent the native people gaining access to the facility and these proved successful until total war ensued. The invaders used a mutated virus to depopulate the area, but it spread planet wide, and eventually mutated again to eliminate the invaders themselves. It was not known that one of the guardians was still functional until you came across it.

'Your handling of the situation showed much ingenuity and careful thought. The remaining guardian in the facility is in a dormant state. If you should wish to visit the facility again, it is suggested that you do not attempt to activate the remaining guardian as its control and recognition circuits may have been corrupted over time, and therefore its response may be unpredictable.'

'Wow, that's the longest statement you've ever made.'

'Correction, it is the longest statement made to you.'

'Have there have been others here, working in the complex as I do?'

'Yes.'

'Can you tell me about them please?'

'Not at this point in time. You have much to learn and understand before some data will be meaningful. In the fullness of time, all your questions will be answered.'

'All right, what's the purpose of the complex?'

'To fulfil the third Prime Directive.'

'What the hell's that?' asked Jed, realizing that reality was about to slip away again.

'That too will be exp...'

'OK, OK, I'll have to wait until you think I'm able to understand it. You realize it's bloody frustrating, this waiting bit.'

'It is regrettable, but necessary for your stable mental advancement.'

'OK, try this one. Was the complex here before the invaders and the native peoples?'

'Yes.'

'Then how come they didn't get curious about it, and try to get inside?'

'The complex is impenetrable to all known forces available to other life forms. The natives developed and grew up with the complex, and accepted it as something they could do little about, and so lost interest in it. The invaders, after a preliminary investigation, were more interested *in the pulse crystals.'*

'So the complex has been here for a very long time?'

'Yes. A very long time indeed.'

'And how long is that?'

There was a pause before the answer came back.

'There is some difficulty in translating to your language the concept of time regarding the existence of the complex.'

'Two last questions. Were you responsible for the creation of the warning bangle made by Tree?'

'It was thought sensible to give you some means of detecting danger in an unfamiliar environment, and Tree has the capabilities to provide such a device.'

'It certainly works well, and the idea of it giving out light was pure genius. As Tree now exists, and is growing, what happened to all the other plants and creatures which must have been here to sustain the natives?'

'The balance of life on this planet was in precarious equilibrium, it only needed a small shift in the reciprocal actions between species to cause a general rundown of sustainable energy sources. Once the invaders introduced the mutated virus, that balance was disturbed, and the rundown to extinction began.'

'So, if I hadn't come along, Tree would not exist?'

'Tree would exist in spore form as it has for a very long time. You would not exist in a body if it were not for the spore receiving your life fluid to initiate its development. You and Tree had a synergistic relationship where you both benefited from the interplay between you.'

'You can say that again!'

'There is no purpose in doing so, you heard it the first time.'

'I'll have to be a little more careful how I phrase things,' Jed replied with a grin, 'although I'm getting better at it.'

'It would expedite our communications, and yes, you are.'

He called it a day, leaving the control room for a spell on the tower above his rest room to gather his thoughts.

He was beginning to relax and feel at home, at long last.

The days sped by as Jed settled down to his new work, never tiring or feeling bored as each new situation was a challenge with its own difficulties to solve.

Although the viewer could show him anything he wished to see in the huge sample halls below, he made many personal visits to marvel over the diversity of the creations on display, wondering who had initially designed them.

Despite many carefully contrived questions on the subject, 'it' would not disclose an answer which made any sense to Jed, and it developed into a high pressure game between them. Jed enjoyed it immensely, and he suspected 'it' did as well, although he was unable to elicit a sensible answer on that either.

As time passed, Jed liked to think a personal relationship had grown up between them, as their conversation was certainly on a more friendly level, sometimes 'it' making the odd joke which on occasions he found a bit obscure, but in retrospect turned out to be extremely subtle.

A major challenge to Jed's ability came up some time later, which gave him the opportunity to display his newly acquired skills to the full.

'On your screen Jed, is a planet third in from its sun. Terra forming has been completed, but there is only one main land mass. The oceans are mineral rich, the atmosphere has stabilized, but there has been no spontaneous life formation in the seas. It is suggested that the land mass be broken up to encourage diverse current flows in the ocean, and once animal life has been established and stabilized, a higher form be introduced with increased intelligence potential. Your suggestions are awaited, as usual. It is thought you will get great pleasure from seeding this virgin planet, and your every decision will be followed with interest.'

Jed cranked up the magnification of the screen until he could see the land in fine detail. There were mountain ranges, which indicated tectonic plate movement, and that could be utilized to split up the land mass into smaller sections by rupturing the sub mantle. A close inspection of the waters revealed a plentiful supply of nutrients, and he would have expected to see some simple life forms present. As there were clouds, the natural lightning should have brought about simple and then complex proteins, but they were unexpectedly absent. Jed began working out a selection of organisms which would suit the environment, and in time mutate, to fill every little niche on the planet below. Natural selection by environmental change would bring about strong species lines, and from these he could either mould or even introduce, the senior species which 'it' had suggested.

CENTRAL CONTROL. (executive statement)

The visitor has passed all tests and is considered most suitable for the project. It shall be instated as Implementor for the sector.

SECTOR CONTROL. (report)

The Implementor looked down upon the planet, and upon the waters of the planet, and saw that they were good, and were rich in nutrients. And he looked upon the land and upon the mountains he had brought about, and saw that they too, were good, and were ready for life. And so he brought together a great collection of his choice, and he did visit it upon the land, and upon the waters of the land, and it did flourish exceedingly. After six time periods, the Implementor did rest from his work, for it was a mighty work, and did look upon all that he had wrought, and was greatly pleased.

The End

**More from sci-fi-cafe.com
by David Reynolds-Moreton**

Anthology of Futures
Anthology of Possibilities
Divergence
Enslavement
Exchange Rate
Extreme Difference
Flight of the Tristan
Fully Guaranteed
Greenways
Inheritance
Light Quest
The Martian Enigma
The Power Seeds
The Seed Garden
The Single Twin
The Sweepers
The Tribe
Transplant
Of Wood, Metal and Glass